This collection of original short stories by some of the masters of modern fantasy brings to *Unicorn* the work of Robert Silverberg, William Horwood, J. G. Ballard, Angela Carter and Brian Aldiss amongst others. Included also in the anthology are stories by Joy Chant, Christopher Evans, Ian Watson, John Grant and Steve Rasnic Tem.

This is the first of two books of short stories for *Unicorn*.

Lands of Never

an anthology of modern fantasy

edited by

MAXIM JAKUBOWSKI

London
UNWIN PAPERBACKS
Boston   Sydney

First published by Unwin Paperbacks 1983

Unwin® Paperbacks
40 Museum Street, London WC1A 1LU, UK

Unwin Paperbacks
Park Lane, Hemel Hempstead, Herts HP2 4TE, UK

George Allen & Unwin Australia Pty Ltd
8 Napier Street, North Sydney, NSW 2060, Australia

ISBN 0 04 823239 4

Typeset in 10 on 11½ point Imprint by Computape (Pickering) Ltd
and printed in Great Britain
by Guernsey Press Co. Ltd, Guernsey, Channel Islands

Contents

Dancers in the Time-Flux   *Robert Silverberg*   *page* 3

The Museum Bell   *William Horwood*   23

The Coming of the Starborn   *Joy Chant*   47

Report on an Unidentified
    Space Station   *J. G. Ballard*   67

The Rites of Winter   *Christopher Evans*   75

In the Mirror of the Earth   *Ian Watson*   87

When All Else Fails   *John Grant*   103

When Coyote Takes Back The World   *Steve Rasnic Tem*   123

The Bridegroom   *Angela Carter*   137

The Girl Who Sang   *Brian W. Aldiss*   147

A popular and once prolific American writer, Robert Silverberg has recently enjoyed great acclaim for his best-selling fantasy volumes about the multi-coloured, gaudy world of Majipoor: *Lord Valentine's Castle* and *The Majipoor Chronicles*. His main claim to fame has, however, been in the field of science fiction where he has won most of the major awards available. A list of his titles could stretch almost as long as his story, but pride of place must be given to *Son of Man* (1971), a surreal evolutionary view of the far future. *Dancers in the Time-Flux* marks a return to this strange and wonderful environment.

Dancers in the Time-Flux

Robert Silverberg

Under a warm golden wind from the west Bhengarn the Traveller moves steadily onward towards distant Crystal Pond, his appointed place of metamorphosis. The season is late. The swollen scarlet sun clings close to the southern hills. Bhengarn's body – a compact silvery tube supported by a dozen pairs of sturdy three-jointed legs – throbs with the need for transformation. And yet the Traveller is unhurried. He has been bound on this journey for many hundreds of years. He has traced across the face of the world a glistening trail that zigzags from zone to zone, from continent to continent, and even now still glimmers behind him with a cold brilliance like a thread of bright metal stitching the planet's haunches. For the past decade he has patiently circled Crystal Pond at the outer end of a radial arm one-tenth the diameter of the Earth in length; now, at the prompting of some interior signal, he has begun to spiral inwards upon it.

The path immediately before him is bleak. To his left is a district covered by furry green fog; to his right is a region of pale crimson grass sharp as spikes and sputtering with a sinister hostile hiss; straight ahead a road-bed of black clinkers and ashen crusts leads down a shallow slope to the Plain of Teeth, where menacing porcellaneous outcroppings make the wayfarer's task a taxing one. But such obstacles mean little to Bhengarn. He is a Traveller, after all. His body is superbly designed to carry him through all difficulties. And in his journeys he has been in places far worse than this.

Elegantly he descends the pathway of slag and cinders. His many feet are tough as annealed metal, sensitive as the most alert antennae. He tests each point in the road for stability and support, and scans the thick layer of ashes for concealed enemies. In this way he moves easily and swiftly towards the plain, holding his long abdomen safely above the cutting edges of the cold volcanic matter over which he walks.

As he enters the Plain of Teeth he sees a new annoyance: an Eater commands the gateway to the plain. Of all the forms of human life – and the Traveller has encountered virtually all of them in his wanderings, Eaters, Destroyers, Skimmers, Interceders, and the others – Eaters seem to him the most tiresome, mere noisy monsters. Whatever philosophical underpinnings form the rationale of their bizarre way of life are of no interest to him. He is wearied by their bluster and offended by their gross appetites.

All the same he must get past this one to reach his destination. The huge creature stands straddling the path with one great meaty leg at each edge and the thick fleshy tail propping it from behind. Its steely claws are exposed, its fangs gleam, driblets of blood from recent victims stain its hard reptilian hide. Its chilly inquisitive eyes, glowing with demonic intelligence, track Bhengarn as the Traveller draws near.

The Eater emits a boastful roar and brandishes its many teeth.

'You block my way,' Bhengarn declares.

'You state the obvious,' the Eater replies.

'I have no desire for an encounter with you. But my destiny draws me towards Crystal Pond, which lies beyond you.'

'For you,' says the Eater, 'nothing lies beyond me. Your destiny has brought you to a termination today. We will collaborate, you and I, in the transformation of your component molecules.'

From the spiracles along his sides the Traveller releases a thick blue sigh of boredom. 'The only transformation that waits for me is the one I will undertake at Crystal Pond. You and I have no transaction. Stand aside.'

The Eater roars again. He rocks slightly on his gigantic claws and swishes his vast saurian tail from side to side. These are the preliminaries to an attack, but in a kind of ponderous courtesy he seems to be offering Bhengarn the opportunity to scuttle back up the ash-strewn slope.

Bhengarn says, 'Will you yield place?'

'I am an instrument of destiny.'

'You are a disagreeable boastful ignoramus,' says Bhengarn calmly, and consumes half a week's energy driving the scimitars of his spirit to the roots of the world. It is not a wasted expense of soul, for the ground trembles, the sky grows dark, the hill behind him creaks and groans, the wind turns purplish and frosty. There is a dull droning sound which the Traveller knows is the song of the time-flux, an unpredictable force that often is liberated at such moments. Despite that, Bhengarn will not relent. Beneath the Eater's splayed claws the fabric of the road ripples. Sour smells rise from sudden crevasses. The enormous beast utters a yipping cry of rage and lashes his tail vehemently against the ground. He sways; he nearly topples; he calls out to Bhengarn to cease his onslaught, but the Traveller knows better than to settle for a half measure. Even more fiercely he presses against the Eater's bulky form.

'This is unfair,' the Eater wheezes. 'My goal is the same as yours: to serve the forces of necessity.'

'Serve them by eating someone else today,' answers Bhengarn curtly, and with a final expenditure of force shoves the Eater to an awkward untenable position that causes it to crash down onto its side. The downed beast, moaning, rakes the air with his claw but does not arise, and as Bhengarn moves briskly past the Eater he observes that fine transparent threads, implacable as stone, have shot forth from a patch of swamp beside the road and are rapidly binding the fallen Eater in an unbreakable net. The Eater howls. Glancing back, Bhengarn notices the threads already cutting their way through the Eater's thick scales like tiny streams of acid. 'So, then,' Bhengarn says, without malice, 'the forces of necessity will be gratified today after all, but not by me. The Eater is to be eaten. It seems that this day *I* prove to be the instrument of destiny.' And without another backward look he passes quickly onward into the plain. The sky regains its ruddy colour, the wind becomes mild once more, the Earth is still. But a release of the time-flux is never without conse-quences, and as the Traveller trundles forwards he perceives some new creature of unfamiliar form staggering through the mists ahead, confused and lost, lurching between the shining lethal formations of the Plain of Teeth in seeming ignorance of the perils they hold. The creature is upright, two-legged, hairy, of archaic appearance. Bhengarn, approaching it, recognises it finally as a primordial human, swept millions of years past its own true moment.

'Have some care,' Bhengarn calls. 'Those teeth can bite!'

'Who spoke?' the archaic creature demands, whirling about in alarm.

'I am Bhengarn the Traveller. I suspect I am responsible for your presence here.'

'Where are you? I see no one! Are you a devil?'

'I am a Traveller, and I am right in front of your nose.'

The ancient human notices Bhengarn, apparently for the first time, and leaps back, gasping. 'Serpent!' he cries. 'Serpent with legs! Worm! Devil!' Wildly he seizes rocks and hurls them at the Traveller, who deflects them easily enough, turning each into a rhythmic juncture of gold and green that hovers, twanging softly, along an arc between the other and himself. The archaic one lifts an immense boulder, but as he hoists it to drop it on Bhengarn he overbalances and his arm flies backwards, grazing one of the sleek teeth behind him. At once the tooth releases a turquoise flare and the man's arm vanishes to the elbow. He sinks to his knees, whimpering, staring bewilderedly at the stump and at the Traveller before him.

Bhengarn says, 'You are in the Plain of Teeth, and any contact with these mineral formations is likely to be unfortunate, as I attempted to warn you.'

He slides himself into the other's soul for an instant, pushing his way past thick encrusted stalagmites and stalactites of anger, fear, outraged pride, pain, disorientation, and arrogance, and discovers himself to be in the presence of one Olivier van Noort of Utrecht, former tavernkeeper at Rotterdam, commander of the voyage of circumnavigation that set forth from Holland on the second day of July 1598 and travelled the entire belly of the world, a man of exceedingly strong stomach and bold temperament, who has experienced much; having gorged on the meat of penguins at Cape Virgines and the isle called Pantagoms; having hunted beasts not unlike stags and buffaloes and ostriches in the cold lands by Magellan's Strait; having encountered whales and parrots and trees whose bark had the bite of pepper; having had strife with the noisome Portugals in Guinea and Brazil; having entered into the South Sea on a day of divers storms, thunders, and lightnings; having taken ships of the Spaniards in Valparaiso and slain many Indians; having voyaged thence to the Isles of Ladrones or Thieves, where the natives bartered bananas, coconuts, and roots for old pieces of iron, overturning their canoes in their greed for metal; having suffered a bloody flux in Manila of eating palmitoes, having captured vessels of China laden with rice and lead; having traded with folk on a ship of the Japans, whose men make themselves bald except for a tuft left in the hinder part of the head, and wield swords which would, with one stroke, cut through three men; having traded also with the bare-breasted women of Borneo, bold and impudent and shrewd, who carry iron-pointed javelins and sharp darts; and having after great privation and the loss of three of his four ships and all but 45 of his 248 men, many of them executed by him or marooned on remote islands for their mutinies but a good number murdered by the treacheries of savage enemies, come again to Rotterdam on 26 August in 1601, bearing little in the way of saleable goods to show for his hardships and calamities. None of this has any meaning to Bhengarn the Traveller except in the broadest, which is to say that he recognises in Olivier van Noort a stubborn and difficult man who has conceived and executed a journey of mingled heroism and foolishness that spanned vast distances, and so they are brothers, of a sort, however millions of years apart. As a fraternal gesture Bhengarn restores the newcomer's arm. That appears to be as bewildering to the other as was its sudden loss. He squeezes it, moves it cautiously back and forth, scoops up a handful of pebbles with it. 'This is Hell, then,' he mutters, 'and you are a demon of Satan.'

'I am Bhengarn the Traveller, bound towards Crystal Pond, and I think that I conjured you by accident out of your proper place in time while seeking to thwart that monster.' Bhengarn indicates the fallen Eater, now half dissolved. The other, who evidently had not looked that way before, makes a harsh choking sound at the sight of the giant creature, which still struggles sluggishly. Bhengarn says, 'The time-flux has seized you and taken you far from home, and there will be no going back for you. I offer regrets.'

'You offer regrets? A worm with legs offers regrets! Do I dream this, or am I truly dead and gone to Hell?'

'Neither one.'

'In all my sailing round the world I never saw a place so strange as this, or the likes of you, or of that creature over yonder. Am I to be tortured, demon?'

'You are not where you think you are.'

'Is this not Hell?'

'This is the world of reality.'

'How far are we, then, from Holland?'

'I am unable to calculate it,' Bhengarn answers. 'A long way, that's certain. Will you accompany me towards Crystal Pond, or shall we part here?'

Noort is silent a moment. Then he says, 'Better the company of demons than none at all, in such a place. Tell me straight, demon: am I to be punished here? I see hell-fire on the horizon. I will find the rivers of fire, snow, toads, and black water, will I not? And the place where sinners are pronged on hooks jutting from blazing wheels? The ladders of red-hot iron, eh? The wicked broiling on coals? And the Arch-Traitor himself, sunk in ice to his chest – he must be near, is he not?' Noort shivers. 'The fountains of poison. The wild boars of Lucifer. The aloes biting bare flesh, the dry winds of the abyss – when will I see them?'

'Look there,' says Bhengarn. Beyond the Plain of Teeth a column of black flame rises into the heavens, and in it dance creatures of a hundred sorts, melting, swirling, coupling, fading. A chain of staring lidless eyes spans the sky. Looping whorls of green light writhe on the mountain-tops. 'Is that what you expect? You will find whatever you expect here.'

'And yet you say this is not Hell?'

'I tell you again, it is the true world, the same into which you were born long ago.'

'And is this Brazil, or the Indies, or some part of Africa?'

'Those names mean little to me.'

'Then we are in the Terra Australis,' says Noort. 'It must be. A land where worms have legs and speak good Dutch, and rocks can bite, and arms once lost can sprout anew – yes, it must surely be the Terra Australis, or else the land of Prester John. Eh? Is Prester John your king?' Noort laughs. He seems to be emerging from his bewilderment. 'Tell me the name of this land, creature, so I may claim it for the United Provinces, if ever I see Holland again.'

'It has no name.'

'No name! No name! What foolishness! I never found a place whose folk had no name for it, not even in the endless South Sea. But I will name it, then. Let this province be called New Utrecht, eh? And all this land, from here to the shores of the South Sea, I annex hereby to the United Provinces in the name of the States-General. You be my witness, creature. Later I will draw up documents. You say I am not dead?'

'Not dead, not dead at all. But far from home. Come, walk beside me, and touch nothing. This is troublesome territory.'

'This is strange and ghostly territory,' says Noort. 'I would paint it, if I could, and then let Mynheer Brueghel look to his fame, and old Bosch as well. Such sights! Were you a prince before you were transformed?'

'I have not yet been transformed,' says Bhengarn. 'That awaits me at Crystal Pond.' The road through the plain now trends slightly uphill; they are advancing into the farther side of the basin. A pale yellow tint comes into the sky. The path here is prickly with little many-faceted insects whose hard sharp bodies assail the Dutchman's bare tender feet. Cursing, he hops in wild leaps, bringing him dangerously close to outcroppings of teeth, and Bhengarn, in sympathy, fashions stout grey boots for him. Noort grins. He gestures toward his bare middle, and Bhengarn clothes him in a shapeless grey robe.

'Like a monk, is how I look!' Noort cries. 'Well, well, a monk in Hell! But you say this is not Hell. And what kind of creature are you, creature?'

'A human being,' says Bhengarn, 'of the Traveller sort.'

'A human being!' Noort booms. He leaps across a brook of sparkling bubbling violet-hued water and waits on the far side as Bhengarn trudges through it. 'A human under an enchantment, I would venture.'

'This is my natural form. Humankind has not worn your guise since long before the falling of the Moon. The Eater you saw was human. Do you see, on yonder eastern hill, a company of Destroyers turning the forest to rubble? They are human.'

'The wolves on two legs up there?'

'Those, yes. And there are others you will see. Awaiters, Breathers, Skimmers – '

'These are mere noises to me, creature. What is human? A Dutchman is human! A Portugal is human! Even a Chinese, a black, a Japonder with a shaven head. But those beasts on yon hill? Or a creature with more legs than I have whiskers. No, Traveller, no! You flatter yourself. Do you happen to know, Traveller, how it is that I am here? I was in Amsterdam, to speak before the Lords Seventeen and the Company in general, to ask for ships to bring pepper from the Moluccas, but they said they would choose Joris van Spilbergen in my place – do you know Spilbergen? I think him much overpraised – and then all went dizzy, as though I had taken too much beer with my gin – and then – then – ah, this is a dream, is it not, Traveller? At this moment I sleep in Amsterdam. I am too old for such drinking. Yet never have I had a dream so real as this, and so strange. Tell me: when you walk, do you move the legs on the right side first, or the left?' Noort does not wait for a reply. 'If you are human, Traveller, are you also a Christian, then?'

Bhengarn searches in Noort's mind for the meaning of that, finds something approximate, and says, 'I make no such claim.'

'Good. Good. There are limits to my credulity. How far is this Crystal Pond?'

'We have covered most of the distance. If I proceed at a steady pace I will come shortly to the land of smoking holes, and not far beyond that is the approach to the Wall of Ice, which will demand a difficult but not impossible ascent, and just on the far side of that I will find the vale that contains Crystal Pond, where the beginning of the next phase of my life will occur.' They are walking now through a zone of sparkling rubbery cones of a bright vermilion colour, from which small green Stangarones emerge in quick succession to chant their one-note melodies. The flavour of a heavy musk hangs in the air. Night is beginning to fall. Bhengarn says, 'Are you tired?'

'Just a little.'

'It is not my custom to travel by night. Does this camp site suit you?' Bhengarn indicates a broad circular depression bordered by tiny volcanic fumaroles. The ground here is warm and spongy, moist, bare of vegetation. Bhengarn extends an excavator claw and pulls free a strip of it, which he hands to Noort, indicating that he should eat. Noort tentatively nibbles. Bhengarn helps himself to some also. Noort, kneeling, presses his knuckles against the ground, makes it yield, mutters to himself, shakes his head, rips off another strip and chews it in wonder. Bhengarn says, 'You find the world much changed, do you not?'

'Beyond all understanding, in fact.'

'Our finest artists have worked on it since time immemorial, making it more lively, more diverting. We think it is a great success. Do you agree?'

Noort does not answer. He is staring bleakly at the sky, suddenly dark and jewelled with blazing stars. Bhengarn realises that he is searching for patterns, navigators' signs. Noort frowns, turns round and round to take in the full circuit of the heavens, bites his lip, finally lets out a low groaning sigh and says, 'I recognise nothing. Nothing. This is not the northern sky, this is not the southern sky, this is not any sky I can understand.' Quietly he begins to weep. After a time he says sombrely, 'I was not the most adept of navigators, but I knew something, at least. And I look at this sky and I feel like a helpless babe. All the stars have changed places. Now I see how lost I am, how far from anything I ever knew, and once it gave me great pleasure to sail under strange skies, but not now, not here, because these skies frighten me and this land of demons offers me no peace. I have never wept, do you know that, creature, never, not once in my life! But Holland – my house, my tavern, my church, my sons, my pipe – where is Holland? Where is everything I knew? The skies above Magellan's Strait were not the thousandth part so strange as this.' A harsh heavy sob escapes him, and he turns away, huddling into himself.

Compassion floods Bhengarn for this miserable wanderer. To ease Noort's pain he summons fantasies for him, dredging images from the reservoirs of the ancient man's spirit and hurling them against the sky, building a cathedral of fire in the heavens, and a royal palace, and a great armada of ships with bellying sails and the Dutch flag fluttering, and the watery boulevards of busy Amsterdam and the quiet streets of little Haarlem, and more. He paints for Noort the stars in their former courses, the Centaur, the Swan, the Bear, the Twins. He restores the fallen Moon to its place and by its cold light creates a landscape of time lost and gone, with avenues of heavy-boughed oaks and maples, and drifts of brilliant red and yellow tulips blazing beneath them, and golden roses arching in great bowers over the thick newly mowed lawn. He creates fields of ripe wheat, and haystacks high as barns, and harvesters toiling in the hot sultry afternoon. He gives Noort the aroma of the Sunday feast and the scent of good Dutch gin and the sweet dense fumes of his long clay pipe. Noort nods and murmurs and clasps his hands, and gradually his sorrow ebbs and his weeping ceases, and he drifts off into a deep and easy slumber. The images fade. Bhengarn, who rarely sleeps, keeps watch until first light comes and a flock of fingerwinged birds passes overhead, shouting shrilly, jesting and swooping.

Noort is calm and quiet in the morning. He feeds again on the spongy soil and drinks from a clear emerald rivulet and they move onward towards Crystal Pond. Bhengarn is pleased to have his company. There is something crude and coarse about the Dutchman, perhaps even more so than another of his era might be, but Bhengarn finds that unimportant. He has always preferred companions of any sort to the solitary march, in his centuries of going to and fro upon the Earth. He has travelled with Skimmers and Destroyers, and once a ponderous Ruminant, and even on several occasions visitors from other worlds who have come to sample the wonders of Earth. At least twice Bhengarn has had as his travelling companion a castaway of the time-flux from some prehistoric era, though not so prehistoric as Noort's. And now it has befallen him that he will go to the end of his journey with this rough hairy being from the dawn of humanity's day. So be it. So be it.

Noort says, breaking a long silence as they cross a plateau of quivering gelatinous stuff, 'Were you a man or a woman before the sorcery gave you this present shape?'

'I have always had this form.'

'No. Impossible. You say you are human, you speak my language – '

'Actually, you speak *my* language,' says Bhengarn.

'As you wish. If you are human you must once have looked

like me. Can it be otherwise? Were you born a thing of silvery scales and many legs? I will not believe that.'

'Born?' says Bhengarn, puzzled.

'Is this word unknown to you?'

'Born,' the Traveller repeats. 'I think I see the concept. To *begin*, to *enter*, to *acquire one's shape* – '

'Born,' says Noort in exasperation. 'To come from the womb. To hatch, to sprout, to drop. Everything alive has to be born!'

'No,' Bhengarn says mildly. 'Not any longer.'

'You talk nonsense,' Noort snaps, and scours his throat angrily and spits. His spittle strikes a node of assonance and blossoms into a dazzling mound of green and scarlet jewels. 'Rubies,' he murmurs. 'Emeralds. I could puke pearls, I suppose.' He kicks at the pile of gems and scatters them; they dissolve into spurts of moist pink air. The Dutchman gives himself over to a sullen brooding. Bhengarn does not transgress on the other's taciturnity; he is content to march forward in his steady plodding way, saying nothing.

Three Skimmers appear, prancing, leaping. They are heading to the south. The slender golden-green creatures salute the wayfarers with pulsations of their great red eyes. Noort, halting, glares at them and says hoarsely to Bhengarn, 'These are human beings too?'

'Indeed.'

'Natives of this realm?'

'Natives of this era,' says Bhengarn. 'The latest form, the newest thing, graceful, supple, purposeless.' The Skimmers laugh and transform themselves into shining streaks of light and soar aloft like a trio of auroral rays. Bhengarn says, 'Do they seem beautiful to you?'

'They seem like minions of Satan,' says the Dutchman sourly. He scowls. 'When I awaken I pray I remember none of this. For if I do, I will tell the tale to Willem and Jan and Piet, and they will think I have lost my senses, and mock me. Tell me I dream, creature. Tell me I lie drunk in an inn in Amsterdam.'

'It is not so,' Bhengarn says gently.

'Very well. Very well. I have come to a land where every living thing is a demon or a monster. That is no worse, I suppose, than a land where everyone speaks Japanese and worships stones. It is a world of wonders, and I have seen more than my share. Tell me, creature, do you have cities in this land?'

'Not for millions of years.'

'Then where do the people live?'

'Why, they live where they find themselves! Last night we lived where the ground was food. Tonight we will settle by the Wall of Ice. And tomorrow – '

'Tomorrow,' Noort says, 'we will have dinner with the Grand Diabolus and dance in the Witches' Sabbath. I am prepared, just as I was prepared to sup with the penguin-eating folk of the Cape, that stood six cubits high. I will be surprised by nothing.' He laughs. 'I am hungry, creature. Shall I tear up the earth again and stuff it down?'

'Not here. Try those fruits.'

Luminous spheres dangle from a tree of golden limbs. Noort plucks one, tries it unhesitatingly, claps his hands, takes three more. Then he pulls a whole cluster free, and offers one to Bhengarn, who refuses.

'Not hungry?' the Dutchman asks.

'I take my food in other ways.'

'Yes, you breathe it in from flowers as you crawl along, eh? Tell me, Traveller: to what end is your journey? To discover new lands? To fulfil some pledge? To confound your enemies? I doubt it is any of these.'

'I travel out of simple necessity, because it is what my kind does, and for no special purpose.'

'A humble wanderer, then, like the mendicant monks who serve the Lord by taking to the highways?'

'Something like that.'

'Do you ever cease your wanderings?'

'Never yet. But cessation is coming. At Crystal Pond I will become my utter opposite, and enter the Awaiter tribe, and be made immobile and contemplative. I will root myself like a vegetable, after my metamorphosis.'

Noort offers no comment on that. After a time he says, 'I knew a man of your kind once. Jan Huyghen van Linschoten of Haarlem, who roamed the world because the world was there to roam, and spent his years in the India of the Portugals and wrote it all down in a great vast book, and when he had done that went off to Novaya Zemlya with Barents to find the chilly way to the Indies, and I think would have sailed to the Moon if he could find the pilot to guide him. I spoke with him once. My own travels took me farther than Linschoten, do you know? I saw Borneo and Java and the world's hinder side, and the thick Sargasso Sea. But I went with a purpose other than my own amusement or the gathering of strange lore, which was to buy pepper and cloves, and gather Spanish gold, and win my fame and comfort. Was that so wrong, Traveller? Was I so unworthy?' Noort chuckles. 'Perhaps I was, for I brought home neither spices nor gold nor most of my men, but only the fame of having sailed around the world. I think I understand you, Traveller. The spices go into a cask of meat and are eaten and gone; the gold is only yellow metal; but so long as there are Dutchmen, no one will forget that Olivier van Noort, the tavernkeeper of Rotterdam, strung a line around the middle of the world. So long as there are Dutchmen.' He laughs. 'It is folly to travel for profit. I will travel for wisdom from now on. What do you say, Traveller? Do you applaud me?'

'I think you are already on the proper path,' says Bhengarn. 'But look, look there: the Wall of Ice.'

Noort gasps. They have come around a low headland and are confronted abruptly by a barrier of pure white light, as radiant as a mirror at noon, that spans the horizon from east to west and rises skyward like an enormous palisade filling half the heavens. Bhengarn studies it with respect and admiration. He has known for hundreds of years that he must ascend this wall if he is to reach Crystal Pond, and that the wall is formidable; but he has seen no need before now to contemplate the actualities of the problem, and now he sees that they are significant.

'Are we to ascend that?' Noort asks.

'I must. But here, I think, we shall have to part company.'

'The throne of Lucifer must lie beyond that icy rampart.'

'I know nothing of that,' says Bhengarn, 'but certainly Crystal Pond is on the farther side, and there is no other way to reach it but to climb the wall. We will camp tonight at its base, and in the morning I will begin my climb.'

'Is such a climb possible?'

'It will have to be,' Bhengarn replies.

'Ah. You will turn yourself to a puff of light like those others we met, and shoot over the top like some meteor. Eh?'

'I must climb,' says Bhengarn, 'using one limb after another, and taking care not to lose my grip. There is no magical way of making this ascent.' He sweeps aside fallen branches of a glowing blue-limbed shrub to make a camp site for them. To Noort he says, 'Before I begin the ascent tomorrow I will instruct you in the perils of the world, for your protection on your future wanderings. I hold myself responsible for your presence here and I would not have you harmed once you have left my side.'

Noort says, 'I am not yet planning to leave your side. I mean to climb that wall alongside you, Traveller.'

'It will not be possible for you.'

'I will make it possible. That wall excites my spirit. I will conquer it as I conquered the storms of the Strait and the fevers of the Sargasso. I feel I should go with you to Crystal Pond, and pay my farewells to you there, for it will bring me luck to mark the beginning of my solitary journey by witnessing the end of yours. What do you say?'

'I say wait until the morning,' Bhengarn answers, 'and see the wall at close range, before you commit yourself to such mighty resolutions.'

During the night a silent lightstorm plays overhead; twisting, turbulent spears of blue and green and violet radiance clash in the throbbing sky, and an undulation of the atmosphere sends alternating waves of hot and cool air racing down from the Wall of Ice. The time-flux blows, and frantic figures out of forgotten eras are swept by now far aloft, limbs churning desperately, eyes rigid with astonishment. Noort sleeps through it all, though from time to time he stirs and mutters and clenches his fists. Bhengarn ponders his obligations to the Dutchman, and by the coming of the sharp blood-hued dawn he has arrived at an idea. Together they advance to the edge of the Wall; together they stare upwards at that vast vertical field of shining whiteness, smooth as stone. Hesitantly Noort touches it with his fingertip, and hisses at the coldness of it. He turns his back to it, paces, folds and unfolds his arms.

He says finally, 'No man of woman born could achieve the

summit of that wall. But is there not some magic you could work, Traveller, that would enable me to make the ascent?'

'There is one. But I think you would not like it.'

'Speak.'

'I could transform you – for a short time, only a short time, no longer than the time it takes to climb the wall – into a being of the Traveller form. Thus we could ascend together.'

Noort's eyes travel quickly over Bhengarn's body – the long tubular serpentine thorax, the tapering tail, the multitude of powerful little legs – and a look of shock and dismay and loathing comes over his face for an instant, but just an instant. He frowns. He tugs at his heavy lower lip.

Bhengarn says, 'I will take no offence if you refuse.'

'Do it.'

'You may be displeased.'

'Do it! The morning is growing old. We have much climbing to do. Change me, Traveller. Change me quickly.' A shadow of doubt crosses Noort's features. 'You will change me back, once we reach the top?'

'It will happen of its own accord. I have no power to make a permanent transformation.'

'Then do what you can, and do it now!'

'Very well,' says Bhengarn, and the Traveller, summoning his fullest force, drains metamorphic energies from the planets and the stars and a passing comet, and focuses them and hurls them at the Dutchman, and there is a buzzing and a droning and a shimmering and when it is done a second Traveller stands at the foot of the Wall of Ice.

Noort seems thunderstruck. He says nothing; he does not move; only after a long time does he carefully lift his frontmost left limb and swing it forwards a short way and put it down. Then the one opposite it; then several of the middle limbs; then, growing more adept, he manages to move his entire body, adopting a curious wriggling style, and in another moment he appears to be in control. 'This is passing strange,' he remarks at length. 'And yet it is almost like being in my own body, except that everything has been changed. You are a mighty wizard, Traveller. Can you show me now how to make the ascent?'

'Are you ready so soon?'

'I am ready,' Noort says.

So Bhengarn demonstrates, approaching the wall, bringing his penetrator claws into play, driving them like pitons into the ice, hauling himself up a short distance, extending the claws, driving them in, pulling upward. He has never climbed ice before, though he has faced all other difficulties the world has to offer, but the climb, though strenuous, seems manageable enough. He halts after a few minutes and watches as Noort, clumsy but determined in his altered body, imitates him, scratching and scraping at the ice as he pulls himself up the face until they are side by side. 'It is easy,' Noort says.

And so it is, for a time, and then it is less easy, for now they hang high above the valley and the midday sun has melted the surface of the wall just enough to make it slick and slippery, and a terrible cold from within the mass of ice seeps outwards into the climbers, and even though a Traveller's body is a wondrous machine fit to endure anything, this is close to the limit. Once Bhengarn loses his purchase, but Noort deftly claps a claw to the middle of his spine to hold him firmly until he has dug in again; and not much later the same happens to Noort, and Bhengarn grasps him. As the day wanes they are so far above the ground that they can barely make out the treetops below, and yet the top of the wall is too high to see. Together they excavate a ledge, burrowing inwards to rest in a chilly nook, and at dawn they begin again, Bhengarn's sinuous body winding upwards over the rim of their little cave and Noort following with less agility. Upwards and upwards they climb, never pausing and saying little, through a day of warmth and soft perfumed breezes and through a night of storms and falling stars, and then through a day of turquoise rain, and through another day and a night and a day and then they are at the top, looking out across the broad unending field of ferns and bright blossoms that covers the summit's flat surface, and as they move inwards from the rim Noort lets out a cry and stumbles forwards, for he has resumed his ancient form. He drops to his knees and sits there panting, stunned, looking in confusion at his fingernails, at his knuckles, at the hair on the backs of his hands, as though he has never seen such things before. 'Passing strange,' he says softly.

'You are a born Traveller,' Bhengarn tells him.

They rest a time, feeding on the sparkling four-winged fruits that sprout in that garden above the ice. Bhengarn feels an immense calmness now that the climax of his peregrination is upon him. Never had he questioned the purpose of being a Traveller, nor has he had regret that destiny gave him that form, but now he is quite willing to yield it up.

'How far to Crystal Pond?' Noort asks.

'It is just over there,' says Bhengarn.

'Shall we go to it now?'

'Approach it with great care,' the Traveller warns. 'It is a place of extraordinary power.'

They go forward; a path opens for them in the swaying grasses and low fleshy-leaved plants; within minutes they stand at the edge of a perfectly circular body of water of unfathomable depth and of a clarity so complete that the reflections of the sun can plainly be seen on the white sands of its infinitely distant bed. Bhengarn moves to the edge and peers in, and is pervaded by a sense of fulfilment and finality.

Noort says, 'What will become of you here?'

'Observe,' says Bhengarn.

He enters Crystal Pond and swims serenely towards the farther shore, an enterprise quickly enough accomplished. But before he has reached the midpoint of the pond a tolling sound is heard in the air, as of bells of the most pure quality, striking notes without harmonic overtones. Sudden ecstasy engulfs him as he becomes aware of the beginning of his transformation: his body flows and streams in the flux of life, his limbs fuse, his soul expands. By the time he comes forth on the edge of the pond he has become something else, a great cone of passive flesh, which is able to drag itself no more than five or six times its own length from the water, and then sinks down on the sandy surface of the ground and begins the process of digging itself in. Here the Awaiter Bhengarn will settle, and here he will live for centuries of centuries, motionless, all but timeless, considering the primary truths of being. Already he is gliding into the earth.

Noort gapes at him from the other side of the pond.

'Is this what you sought?' the Dutchman asks.

'Yes. Absolutely.'

'I wish you farewell and Godspeed, then!' Noort cries.

'And you – what will become of you?'

Noort laughs. 'Have no fears for me! I see my destiny unfolding!'

Bhengarn, nestled now deep in the ground, enwombed by the earth, immobile, established already in his new life, watches as Noort strides boldly to the water's edge. Only slowly, for an Awaiter's mind is less agile than a Traveller's, does Bhengarn comprehend what is to happen.

Noort says, 'I've found my vocation again. But if I'm to travel, I must be equipped for travelling!'

He enters the pond, swimming in broad awkward splashing strokes, and once again the pure tolling sound is evoked, a delicate carillon of crystalline transparent tone, and there is sudden brilliance in the pond as Noort sprouts the shining scales of a Traveller, and the jointed limbs, and the strong thick tail. He scuttles out on the far side wholly transformed.

'Farewell!' Noort cries joyously.

'Farewell,' murmurs Bhengarn the Awaiter, peering out from the place of his long repose as Olivier van Noort, all his legs ablaze with new energy, strides away vigorously to begin his second circumnavigation of the globe.

I am particularly pleased to include in *Lands of Never* what is the first short story of William Horwood, the celebrated author of the animal fantasy *Duncton Wood* and the impressive *The Stonor Eagles*. A former journalist on the *Daily Mail*, Horwood here offers us a quiet but powerful tale about the influence of a fascinating object on the minds of three men.

The Museum Bell

William Horwood

Maybe they're right to think me drunk. But Assistant Keepers have a right to get drunk one night a year, and the Far Eastern Department's Christmas party has always been the best at which to do it.

As a matter of fact I *am* drunk. I am also listening over the sound of their chatter and laughter for a certain sound, far beyond the doors of the Department, down past the offices and out into the silent darkened corridors of the Museum itself.

I have been beginning to hear it for a long time now, and so beginning to understand the things they said. Some nights when I've finished work I've made a detour through the silent Museum just to stand where they both used to stand on this same night each year.

Far Eastern's always been the best party, always will be. It's the only office Christmas party I've ever heard of that's endowed, and whose funds are index-linked. £100 for drink and eats at 1965 prices, which is too much. No wonder Assistant Keepers get drunk.

I came in 1967, very junior, straight down from Cambridge. They put me into Twentieth Century Drawings and there I still am, but more senior now; and listening. If that sound is what I think it is – and no I don't reply when someone asks me some bloody silly thing, begging your pardon – if it *is*, then I know why I'm frightened. Dammit all, I want to cry, so I'm blundering through them muttering about feeling sick which isn't true at all. Just small and frightened, because I'm beginning to hear it now, and if they can't they must be bloody deaf.

Far Eastern's party is endowed because in 1965 Edvard Rothenstein, the not-so-famous-then great multinational industrialist, gave John Gardner, then Keeper of the Department, a cheque sufficient (at that time, before inflation) to endow an annual party. Rothenstein has topped it up occasionally since.

He also in that year began to come to the party, tall and impressive, quite literally above the Museum gossip and the chitter-chatter. Each year, on that night, at about 10.00, when hardly anyone was noticing, he and old John Gardner wended their way through the same dark corridors I'm entering now, glass in hand (as I have now), to stand together and in silence by the great Tibetan bell that rests mutely in a corner of the Charles II staircase in the West Wing, beyond Medieval armour.

I know all this because I followed them. You see, unlike some in the Museum, I'm interested in people, but then I'm one of the few who deal in objects made by living hands.

True, a lot of the objects the Museum buys on my advice are by dead hands. Picasso, Bague, Giacometti; all dead. But a lot of it – Hockney, Dine, Moore – they live. Good buyers of art must like people.

I often thought that old man Gardner, the greatest and most loved Keeper we have had in living memory, ought to have been in Twentieth Century Drawings and not the mostly distant past of Far Eastern. He knew people. You could tell it from the way he handled an object he liked, with gentleness, with care, with excitement, and always with love.

Some of us juniors used to make any excuse to watch John Gardner study an object and tell us about it, just as junior balletines at the Bolshoi Ballet watch senior students going through their paces.

So, I was curious about the mystery of the connection between him and Rothenstein. There *was* a mystery because no one else, none bar none, ever got invited to a Museum Christmas party unless they were Staff, Committee or Patron. Rothenstein was none of those. He was an industrialist with no known connection with the Museum. I know because I checked. It behoves Assistants when they come to the Museum to check out who is who. They may not like people, but it pays to know them.

If that mystery was all I had to go on it would not have been enough to bother with, beyond an idle moment or two's gossip with colleagues around Christmas time when the two filled each other's glasses and talked about God knows what in a corner away from the rest. But it was more than that. Anyone with a mite of sensitivity could feel a bond between them, different though they were. Gardner thin and donnish, his old grey suits the stuff of which emeritus fellows of Cambridge colleges are made; Rothenstein towering above him, lean and healthier looking.

I first noticed them disappearing together the first year I was there, in 1967. In 1969 I followed them.

They went down past the Abyssinian Marbles; left at Indian Miniatures; right and then left through Room XII; across into the Long Corridor towards the West Wing, and so to the top of the Charles II staircase. (It's nineteenth century in fact. So called because of the bust at its foot. It's Staircase D on the new guide.)

Then they wandered down the stairs, talking, as I remember, about medieval currency and inflation from which subject – and I remember Rothenstein's words precisely – they got onto medieval crime. His voice carried up to the marble balustrade over which I was slyly leaning (glass also in hand, and relatively drunk) as he said, 'The murder rate in Oxford in 1410 was nine times higher than it is in Los Angeles today.'

Then they fell silent but by craning round at a dangerous angle I could see they were standing by an object which I had never really noticed until that moment: the Tibetan bell, object MN 42529CD.

They stood in silence before it for a very long time and it seemed to me then, as it has often since, that there is something about that bell that attracts a peaceful darkness. In the black patina of its ancient bronze, light seems to fade to nothingness, the effort of striving goes, and the way is open for the spirit to be itself.

Such a feeling is, of course, quite unconsciously arrived at and the moment it is articulated it begins to fade, and the sounds of life – in this case a distant and ongoing Christmas party – begin to intrude again. At that moment, as I watched them, I felt what I should have felt long before, that *I* was intruding. So silently a floor above them, I left.

I often wondered in the three or four years after whether they ever became aware that I had been tacked on to their arcane ritual by my own curiosity. Each Christmas I would follow them out of the Far Eastern party, delighting to take a separate route from them and arriving as nearly at the same time as they did, only above where they stood: to share with them their strange secret.

I read about Rothenstein in the papers – who did not as the era of takeovers began in the 'sixties? – but I never spoke more than a courtesy word to him at those parties. Indeed, he seemed to me then of secondary importance in finding the solution of whatever mystery it was that took them on their annual pilgrimage to a silent bell.

As the years passed I grew close to John Gardner, then getting older and nearing retirement, and his liking for me was sometimes commented on with envy by other Assistants. He would often seek me out at lunch-times in the staff canteen and sit opposite me saying, 'All well? All's fine is it on the Third Floor?' – which is where Twentieth Century Drawings has both its offices and its collection. He was never much interested in conversation but I sensed that in me he found a silent companionship which he liked. He ate in a slow and deliberate way, eyeing the salads that he usually chose to have with the same affectionate curiosity that he eyed Far Eastern objects. He drank his tea slowly after his main course choosing that moment to survey others in the canteen and had a partiality for shortcake biscuits. We rarely really talked at these meals. He really needed the medium of an object in his hands to open up.

One year, as Christmas approached and the secretaries were putting up Christmas decorations in the canteen, quite impromptu and without thought, I asked him as we drank our tea: 'What is Edvard Rothenstein's importance to the Museum, Sir?' (We all called him Sir, and without resentment. One felt that he had earned it.)

He was silent for a long time, gazing up to the skylights high above the canteen hall, which were already dark with early December storms even though it was midday. Great dark clouds billowed above our heads.

'It is rare in life to be a witness at the moment a man's life is changed,' he replied. Then he munched hard on a shortcake biscuit and changed the subject to something inconsequential: myself.

Somehow, the reply, for all its mystery and indirectness, made me feel I had his confidence. Certainly I sensed that he understood that I had seen what others had not seemed to. Most important of all, I knew he didn't mind. Such a flood of feelings all at once! He seemed old sitting there across from me, asking polite questions to courteously block my trespassing with words where our spirits could much better go.

That was the first time I really asked his advice. 'All's well is it?' he had asked after his curious reply to my question to change the subject: 'All's well?' But no, Sir, it wasn't all well.

Yet were my frustrations and doubts about staying in the Museum, for all my success in it, any different from any other assistant who felt he was rising fast into a cul-de-sac? Was it normal in an Assistant to feel that a study of objects was an escape from people? These thoughts, no doubt jumbled and incoherent and not the thing to reveal to a Keeper, did not provoke an obviously comforting response. John Gardner munched at his biscuit, drank his tea, and said non-committally, 'Ah! Yes!' Yet in his presence I found comfort, and he continued to seek me out.

It was a year after that first real exchange between us, and only a few months prior to John Gardner's retirement, that the Christmas party came, when I learnt the nature of the bond between them. The hour had come when Rothenstein and Gardner left the room alone and perhaps the knowledge that it was Gardner's last Christmas party put into me the excitement, and the courage, to impel me to do what I did.

I followed them both as usual, just a little tipsy perhaps, but rather serious about this particular approach to the bell.

Why were my feet so sure, my walk so certain, my mind so at peace? Why did I not stop above as in the past and watch from the shadows their annual moment of silence? Why did I see them both below and walk down to them? What is it tells you when the moment's right? If we could speak *that* language all the time, what need would we have of words?

I smiled at them as I came down to where they stood before the bell. Gardner nodded as if he understood, or at least expected me. To my surprise Edvard Rothenstein spoke my name, prefacing it with a Mister. He obviously knew about me, and

from the brief words of introduction we spoke I realised he knew
a great deal about the Museum, and something to do about its
Twentieth Century collection.

I remember standing in silence with them simply staring into
the bell's dark depths of configuration and embossment and
thinking of nothing much as my eyes stayed on one point but my
head seemed to move about a little.

'Why do you both come to this bell every year?' I asked
outright.

Rothenstein laughed aloud, his laughter rising into the marble
balustrades and corridors above us; while John Gardner supped
at his glass of red wine smiling in a quite delightful way. I
confessed that I had long been following them. Then one of
them began and the other continued, and together they told me
why they came to the bell.

It was October 1939 and Hattie Rothenstein and her nephew,
Edvard, were lucky to get into the Museum at all. The authorities were already evacuating its most vulnerable and valuable
objects to the protection of slate mines in North Wales and great
sections of it were closed now, the echoing corridors full of the
sound of men's voices and the clutter of moving. The air carried
the smell of dust-sheets and change.

But security was different then, easier, and the Warder at the
entrance saw only the beginnings of a look of disappointment on
the mother's face (as he supposed her to be) before he said, 'All
right, love, I suppose it'll be all right, but don't go through any
of the barriers.'

So they had the Museum almost to themselves; she pale, and
her face drawn with a terrible tiredness, and he expressionless
and small.

She wanted him to see the heritage of the country that had
taken them in to begin to build something to replace the home
and the family they had left behind in Germany. Their departure had been quite sudden. Her elder sister had heard there was
a chance of seats on a train into Belgium and had persuaded
Hattie to take her youngest boy, Edvard. Had her husband
known it would have been against his wishes but some terrible
dread of what was to come made her do it. A dark overcoat,

warm boots and a little leather bag, and he stood staring up at her, his hand in his aunt's. His two brothers, his sister, his father, his grandmother and the rest of the great family were left behind. It was all a secret, so he never said goodbye. They became shadows in his mind. His first childhood memory was of a train journey through tunnels of fear and across chasms of dread and the great black side of a boat. The sea out of which it rose from far below the harbour wall was oily and dark, and he was afraid of it. He began to learn English the first day he arrived: 'port' was the first word he ever spoke in English, 'train' the second.

He was shocked into a defensive silence by the sudden flight, and the smile he had had, and which had so often been remarked on by relatives and family friends, was gone. He was small and serious and it became hard to say what he was thinking. He always looked much older than his age.

Letters, contact with other Jewish refugees from Germany, the search for news, the reading of newspapers for hope: these were what preoccupied Hattie's mind. The intensity she put into Edvard was a reflection of the love she could not give or receive from doomed relatives. Should she ever had left? From some instinctual understanding of the nature of the shock Edvard was suffering she tried to give him a new base.

When she heard that the Museum was being progressively evacuated because of the danger of bombing she brought him down to London that he might see with his own eyes the richness of the place they had come to.

They wandered the corridors, she talking a little about those objects she had something to say about, Edvard listening and saying nothing. She hoped he would respond to something, but not even the Egyptian sculptures seemed to interest him, nor the mummies, nor the huddled and dried body of an ancient burial.

In some rooms there were no lights and the gloom was deep between cases and objects. In others, the objects were shrouded. Corridors and doors, great cases and grim glass, a few steps could traverse the centuries from Egyptian to Anglo-Saxon, and from that to Far Eastern. A few steps, a lingering, and sudden absorption in some strange object behind glass, and a boy is easily lost.

'Edvard?' She called his name softly so as not to disturb the silence too much. But disappearing footsteps that might have been a boy's were the only reply.

'Edvard! Edvard!' Hattie Rothenstein smiled a little. He was safe sure enough . . . and yet she did not like him gone from her at all. Not now. So she began to search.

Edvard wandered down the Long Corridor, past Medieval metalwork, to the foot of the Charles II staircase and looked up at the spiralling balustrades above. He began to ascend the wide staircases; they were so wide at the turns that he had to take two paces before rising up one step.

Then he saw the bell. Bigger than him then, mute and silent as he was, and its embossments and black patina far more ancient. He reached out a hand to touch it. He knew it was a bell.

How long he stood there staring he never knew but he came out of his stare when he heard, somewhere below and in the distance, his aunt's voice: 'Edvard!' Then, almost simultaneously a great tall man came down the stairs towards him, smiling. Edvard was not afraid of him.

'*Wieso kann Man die Glocke nicht läuten lassen?*' It was the kind of question he might have asked his father.

'Mmm?' John Gardner did not understand. He must have misheard. The boy repeated whatever it was he had said. It was obviously German – not one of his languages unfortunately.

The boy was pointing at the bell and looking hopeful.

'Edvard!' A woman came panting up the stairs, her face worried. Edvard was standing by the great dark bell, above him were the recesses of a window cut into the marbled angles of the staircase wall and at his side was a tall English-looking man, who was smiling.

'I'm afraid I can't understand what he's asking,' said Gardner. 'Do you speak English?'

Edvard spoke to her. 'Speak English,' she said. 'Ask him in English.'

As Gardner felt embarrassed for the child Edvard looked away from her at the bell, his right foot kicking gently against its impregnable base.

'Can I help?' asked Gardner again.

Hattie Rothenstein turned to him smiling. 'He only wants to ring the bell,' she said ironically.

'Well, I'm sure . . .' And Gardner's mind travelled the corridors and courtyards of the Museum faster than his feet ever could, in search of a bell that the boy might ring, then dismissed the idea as just not possible . . . 'I'm sure if it were possible he might. But it's an object for display, you see . . . it's never been rung . . . it's just an object, a very beautiful bell. From Tibet.' He said this last a little loudly in the direction of the boy's ear, as if it might help him understand. The boy looked miserable and glum like children sometimes do with adults in the Museum. They'd do better taking them to the Science Museum in Kensington. That's where *he* had gone as a child. Or London Zoo. Or something.

The woman turned again to the boy and spoke again in German. Then she added in English, as if she wanted Gardner to know she was telling the boy what she should.

'It's a beautiful object to be looked at by many people. It isn't for ringing any more, Edvard.'

The boy turned away from the bell and looked not at her but at Gardner, his eyes fiercely angry.

'Why?' he shouted in English. He enunciated the word very clearly and it travelled up the staircase and down it, echoing into adjacent Museum rooms. 'Why?'

Afterwards Gardner remembered the anger in the boy and the very reasonable question and the fact that his right hand was stretched out towards the bell as if – and how ridiculous it seemed – the bell was a mute who could not speak in protest and the boy was asking the question on its personal behalf.

Did they really tell me all this? They must have done but I can only remember standing there, all high on wine, and staring at the bell's black shadows as they talked. Which one told me what I don't know, nor why they told me at all. Except that now, walking alone towards the bell, whose dreadful tolling I *can* hear, I wish I could remember more. I wish I understood. I wish I was not afraid.

That wartime incident with the bell seemed to have affected Rothenstein deeply and the silence of the bell became a symbol throughout his childhood and adolescence for all he had lost when his aunt had taken him from Germany.

But it was not an obsession then, merely an image that some-times surfaced in his mind and provoked a mixed response of despair and hope, anger and peace. Once he was being bullied in the locker-room of the private junior school he was sent to in Ealing, London, and lying with his cheek against the wooden locker door, his nose and mouth in the dry dust left by boy's rugger boots, the bell was suddenly there in front of him and he was not afraid. He stood up slowly in a way that the bully, Stiles, could not quite face out, and brushed the dust of his grey flannel shorts and stared round straight into Stiles' eyes. Stiles mum-bled and left, and as Edvard watched him go, the great bell silent in his head, he wanted to cry but he never did.

One half term, at senior school then, his aunt and a man took him down to Brighton beach. Edvard was now rather thin and arrogant. He went off alone, crunching down the pebbles to the sea, conscious that people might be looking at him though in fact few were, and those that did, did so with near indifference. Some public school boy growing up was all they might have thought. Those days sudden angry moods overtook him, though being Edvard he never ever let them show. Power lay in keeping thoughts hidden. His gaze was cold, his eyes intelligent, his body tall and thin. Sudden bleak despair and in his mind the bell again, black and silent. He threw a stone high out to sea, to try and reach where it might be, but the image faded and was gone.

There were many moments like that, but of Edvard and the bell only one thing could be safely said: he was afraid to go and see it again. Really quite afraid. He had never been back to the Museum and the only time he was ever ill at school was when his Form had a trip to see some Viking treasures at the Museum. He was genuinely sick and could not go.

Hattie was one of those who brought her protégés up as Englishmen, though living in Ealing she was in the midst of a Jewish community yet it was little more than a background thing. Something had broken in her as well on that flight from home and whatever hope there had been that their family was alive and might come out one day died in the bleak years after the war as the truth of it all became known. She forbade Edvard from mentioning it. Together they blocked out their past. Her lovers were never Jews. One, even, was a German. Hattie was rather a formidable woman who did things well and whose wishes were commands.

Like aunt, like nephew. Edvard did not choose to go to the university or read for the degree that his school wished. They said he could have gone to Oxford or Cambridge; he should, they said, have read mathematics, at which he was the best the school had had. He might have been as good at any of half a dozen other subjects, arts and science. What he chose to do was a course in business and accountancy at Manchester University. He did very well and though he did the Shell and ICL and Dexion interviews that the university recruitment office arranged, he finally refused to take any advice about jobs. He was offered second interviews and several jobs, he chose instead to work from a seedy little jobbing engineering firm in Manchester, run by a Mr Mandel, on which he had done a personal project on management information systems as part of his course. The company was called Mandel Engineering Ltd and had fixed (and ageing) assets of £257,000 and debts that should have been chased up or written off a long time before; and current liabilities which were beginning to get out of control.

Mr Mandel was the grandson of the founder of the company and his name might now be quite forgotten but for Rothenstein's arrival on his industrial doorstep. For today, of course, Mandel (Holdings) Limited, of which the chief shareholder is Edvard Rothenstein, is one of Britain's few home-based multinational companies which has achieved international recognition. Its company logo – which appears on all stationery company reports, corporate advertising, and private jet – is the image, somewhat modernised by a New York advertising agency graphics department, of a dark and fascinating Tibetan bell.

The company archives would also show, to anyone who delved into them, that Rothenstein did not stay very long with Mandel Engineering after he first joined it in 1955.

He did an MBA at Harvard Business School; he did a spell in the accounts department of John Brown, the engineering company; he did time for Brunner Ltd in Germany and later in London.

He dressed soberly and well, he worked hard, he put on a little weight, he became a corporate man. His base was accountancy and engineering, his prospects ahead of any in his peer group. By the time he was thirty he was being groomed for very senior management indeed.

So why, in 1965, did he leave Brunners and London and return to Manchester and the tawdry little engineering company run by a tired Mr Mandel?

These questions were asked by Rothenstein himself as he stood with his hand on the bell, a drink in his other hand, with John Gardner and myself that strange Christmas party night. Both men smiled with the shared conspiracy of friends who know the answers; but their faces fell serious and just a little awed as they finally told me the answer.

It was 1963 and Rothenstein was still at Brunners when the bell suddenly came back into his life. Remember, he had never dared return to see it since his wartime experience with it.

It was a lovely day in London, the kind when the plane trees suddenly begin to take on their summer colours of silver grey and pale green, and their branches rise into a fresh and hopeful sky beyond the grimed Regency and Victorian buildings. Rothenstein was travelling by cab between the City and the West End for lunch. Kingsway and New Oxford Street were closed to traffic. The taxi took a detour around the Regency squares of central London. It paused at some lights and Edvard found himself staring at the black railings of a Museum he had not dared to visit for over twenty years. Though he had passed it before, yet he had never responded to it as he did now. He was at once afraid and fascinated. Behind the railings the great Corinthian columns rose, pale and light in the weak spring sun. Visitors passed back and forth through the great gates, adults and children. Impulsively Edvard looked away and then looked back, and a terrible longing, the longing that lay behind so much of the feelings behind his serious face, came back a hundred times as strong as it had ever been. He paid off the cab and with thumping heart entered beneath the great black railings and up the great steps to the Museum itself. He had no idea of where to go to find the bell. He asked a young girl in the information desk. She gave him a layout map. 'It's probably the one on the Charles II staircase,' she said. 'It's Tibetan. You can't really miss it, about halfway up.'

Edvard walked the Museum's rooms and corridors feeling at once curious and fearful wondering whether, after so long, he would recognise something. But the Museum was full of light and people, and objects of colour and gold. His memory of it was wartime monochrome, of shadows and polished mahogany cases, and fading handwritten exhibit cards.

But in the Long Corridor, where the light was not so good, and the display remains what it was during the war – Medieval metalwork – a frisson of an old feeling came back and his apprehension redoubled. Ahead the corridor lightened out into a great staircase. He reached it, and knew it, and saw through the balustrades above the black baseline curve of the bell. Then he climbed a few stairs, turned a corner, and was standing before it once again.

He felt a bit of a fool. It was just a bell in a museum resting on a marble floor in the alcove of a great staircase. A card – printed – that identified it as Tibetan, 9th Century AD. He stared at the bell and wanted to touch it. He found himself afraid to. Logic overrode emotion: he touched it and found it rough and cold. He knocked it with his knuckles and it was no different than knocking a wall: no ringing sound.

He stood before it remembering the child he once had been and the question he had asked of the man in the museum: Why can't you ring the bell?

He remembered the frightened boy he once was and in that moment he began that chain of questions that may begin so frail and hesitantly but end so huge and critical. Such questions can seem to break a man; yet may come to give a man his life.

There were, of course, no obvious answers. It was in any case the fact of asking the questions that mattered. But from that visit Rothenstein started to change, and some might say that he began to break down. His work at Brunners became erratic, his mind wandered into topics and feelings he had no logical explanation of or need for. He rowed with his aunt Hattie about his past: what right had she never to speak of it? What had *happened*? Feelings of pride and guilt at his Jewishness; concerns for questions of spirituality which it seemed illogical and unconstructive to ask, but which persisted in asking themselves. Computer print-out of production variances, and his once analytic mind wandered from figures on his office desk into images of God. His sudden crying, his sudden laughter, all out of control now.

He began to visit the Museum quite regularly, and irregularly as well, to seek out the bell and stare at it. And before it there was only one question to ask. 'What would it sound like if it was ever rung?'

It was on one of those visits that John Gardner met him again. It was Rothenstein who recognised Gardner who came down the stairs towards where he stood by the bell. A year before Rothenstein would have done nothing but let the man who looked only very distantly familiar pass him by. But Rothenstein had changed and was more outspoken now. The man looked a Museum type and was carrying a sheaf of very Museum-looking papers.

'They ought to hang it up so it could ring,' said Rothenstein for openers.

Gardner stopped and stared at the young man. He smiled.

'Yes,' he said, 'people do say that. Very difficult in a museum. People will persist in ringing them. We take out the clappers when bells are hung up.'

Rothenstein stared harder trying positively to place the face, the voice, perhaps some chemistry in the way Gardner stood now near him, next to the bell, as they stood together so long before.

'As a matter of fact it was the first thing that ever struck me about this bell – the fact that it should be rung.'

Gardner was silent.

'At the beginning of the war. My aunt brought me. Just before you closed the Museum.'

'Oh, we never entirely closed it. Quite a few things stayed, including this bell, actually. Only the breakables and moveables went, to the slate mines in North Wales.'

It was Rothenstein's turn to be silent.

He sensed that the Museum man was staring at him, as indeed he was. For Gardner was trained in association, in feel, in distant connections between disparate objects and events, in clues and in detection. He wanted to reach out and touch this tall man at his side; to feel his way back to a memory. But failing that, he stared and Rothenstein kept quite silent. Breathless.

'It was 1939,' said Gardner at last, more to himself than to Rothenstein, as if telling himself the facts by slow recall. 'A mother and a son. Foreigners. German immigrants.' He stopped, and then declared, 'My word, I *do* remember. You said just one word I could understand.'

'WHY?' And Rothenstein spoke it out again now, but not as he should have done – quietly and remembering. He spoke it angrily and with accusation. To Rothenstein in that moment Gardner was not a Museum man, or even Gardner, he was in some strange way the power that cast the bell into perpetual silence, the power that drove a little boy from his childhood home.

'Why?' But Rothenstein's voice was quieter now, for he was very close to tears.

In all his life Gardner had handled thousands on thousands of objects, and on just a few occasions, very very few, he had the sense of holding in his hands something far different from the average. Something embued by craftsmanship and language into an object which carries light from one century to another, from an ancient past into a living present. He found he was touching the bell, and in its touch he felt that ancient kind of power.

Gardner stared at the upset man before him and felt again that same embarrassed frustration he had felt decades before when the little boy asked a question he could not understand. He had wanted to help in some way then; he felt he could help now. He moved his hand from the bell and reached out and touched his arm.

'Perhaps it would help if I let you know how the Museum came by the bell, and what its history is. It is easy enough to find out,' he said.

In the event, the discovery of the progeny of the bell made nothing simpler or easier for either Gardner or Rothenstein. The bell had been brought back from India as part of the Collection of Dr R. J. Drew-Yates whose widow gave it to the Museum along with other parts of his estate in 1886. Drew-

Yates' records showed that he had bought it in 1857 from a trader in Delhi for '£10 sterling and eight small ivory objects'. Later research dated the bell as AD 921–968, probably from the Yashan province of south Tibet. The bell was, in short, colonial plunder, and it now rested in the Museum of a very different culture, surrounded in the main by objects in which most visitors were infinitely more interested. It was reasonably out of the way, displayed within the terms of the Drew-Yates bequest, and anyway too much trouble to move.

These facts did not take Gardner long to establish, and he saw Rothenstein a few weeks later to impart them. He did so in the canteen where I had so often had lunch with him. The two men found they had a liking for each other, though at that stage Rothenstein was in such a crisis of life change – or *upset*, as the more prosaic English vocabulary of the Keeper put it – that he was barely aware of Gardner as an individual. At that meeting, too, Rothenstein asked Gardner if it could not be arranged for the bell to be rung. Impossible, was the reply. Pointless and costly. They had a slight argument about it and Rothenstein left. He wrote the day after to apologise.

Keepers are used to individuals attaching themselves obsessively to an object and becoming a thorough nuisance to the Keeper in whose charge the object is. Sadly, such individuals, who may acquire a smattering of period knowledge, usually turn out to be eccentric or positively queer. Yet their letters, and their visits, must be dealt with politely. After all, many of the best collections the Museum had acquired had come from such eccentrics of which the Nineteenth Century British Empire had more than its fair share.

But Gardner's treatment of Rothenstein – who now came almost daily to the Museum to stand and stare at the silent bell – was warm and friendly. He liked the young man. Perhaps there was something in him of the son he had never had. Perhaps it was the occasional flash of humour that crossed Rothenstein's otherwise impassive and unemotional face – as if awakening by slow degrees to the possibility that his growing obsession with the notion of a particular bell being run was, in fact, absurd. But most of all it must have been Rothenstein's frequently expressed belief that the objects in the Museum, including the one on which his attention had now fixed, were made by people who themselves had lived and breathed and suffered as – and how slowly had he grown to see it – he himself had, and still was.

They met occasionally by the bell – indeed Gardner surprised himself by making detours during lunch hours to see if Rothenstein was there and finding himself disappointed that he was not. But he often was, and at one of these meetings Rothenstein, who had begun to read round his subject, asked Gardner what he knew of Buddhist meditation techniques. The answer was quite a lot, in theory, but not a lot in practice.

'The bell probably knows a lot more than either of us,' said Rothenstein, bringing the conversation, as he always did, to the subject of his obsession.

'It's a strange fact that while I have no trouble at all concentrating for long periods on some business problem or other, when it comes to the kind of concentration meditation demands I can last about ten minutes. It is very hard thinking of nothing – you should try it some time, Mr Gardner.'

Gardner laughed. 'If that's what meditation is I do it all the time. It's the best way to evaluate an object, you know, clearing your mind as your hands and senses take it in. The mind only confuses.'

'Well, I've learnt that the hardest thing is to define the problem,' said Rothenstein. 'Once that is done then the solution finds itself. The problem of meditation does not seem to respond to this approach. Somehow or other the bell must know the answer.'

They both fell silent, and Rothenstein was suddenly depressed. With barely a word more he walked away.

It was November now and such meetings had been going on for several months. Each time Gardner seemed to grow more at peace with himself, more compassionate with his new friend, while Rothenstein grew more distraught, more angry. At one of their meetings he revealed that he had left his job: he was 'thinking' about an offer of work in Manchester. He did not say what it was, and Gardner probably would not have understood in any case.

It was a cold, wet November which brought an early pall of winter over London, a time when maintenance men do indoor jobs. So it was that one day, when the increasingly distracted Rothenstein came to the bell, he found it surrounded by scaffolding and ladders and shrouded in dust-sheets. He had a feeling of *déjà vu*. The walls around the staircase were being decorated. He nearly walked away without a further pause but that something about the shrouded bell held him and something else made a connection in his mind with the scaffolding above. He had that week revisited Manchester and seen again the old-fashioned machinery at Mandel Engineering. Perhaps the image of a chain hoist was still in his mind. But standing there he suddenly saw a way to raise the bell. To raise it and to ring it, just once. To hear its sound in which some answer lay.

Such impulses, made in the flash of a moment, may lead a man to murder or to genius, they say. All the permutations of the act, all the interlocking possibilities and problems, all the ways and all the means: all come together in the mind. So, standing there, Rothenstein saw a way to ring the bell, and in the same instant resolved to see it through.

The difficulties and dangers of the enterprise – to bring hoist gear and props and all the necessary things – did not seem to be a problem, nor the growing eccentricity of the enterprise. He would do it. He would apply to use the Museum Library; he would work late, or at least delay until after the public were no longer admitted into the main Museum. He would leave the library calmly, take a route via the deserted Charles II staircase, arrange a hoist system using the scaffolding that existed, and raise the bell the few inches necessary for it to be rung. He would even bring a hammer to strike it with. No, a wooden mallet would be better.

The fact that people would come running; the fact that he would be caught – these possibilities and repercussions did not cross his obsessed mind. He had finally defined the problem – that the bell must be rung – and effected an instant solution in his mind. And he would do it within a day or two, before the scaffolding was taken down and his opportunity gone. He would do it tomorrow.

We stood by the bell the night they told me all this – Rothenstein, old Gardner and I – and I looked up at the great walls and ceilings above the bell, and the recess of the window over it. I could barely imagine the scaffolding let alone the fact that such an established figure as Rothenstein, head of a multinational corporation and so far as I could tell perfectly normal, was telling me this bizarre story. Yet looking at him then, I saw in his face something of the obsession it must originally have possessed, something of the fixation. And as for Gardner, the earlier smile had gone from his face and that look of awe I had briefly seen before had come back. He was staring at the bell, his wine glass now empty and at rest on one of the stairs, above which the Museum's corridors and rooms disappeared in darkness. Rothenstein continued to talk but quietly as if, even now, years later, he did not believe that whatever it was had happened had really taken place.

Tomorrow came. Rothenstein had made plans well. He carried those things he felt he needed in a bag – the kind of bag no security man would let pass unvetted today. He took his place in the library at the back end of the Museum and did whatever research he had got permission to do – he had asked Gardner to authorise a temporary reader's ticket for him.

It was past 5.30 p.m. and the Museum visitors had left the public rooms outside the library which was filled with the silence of scholarship. Rothenstein was extremely calm. He had in fact been sitting staring at the books he had ordered without reading their print. He had been meditating and somehow it had started to come right. The problem of meditation he was beginning to see is that there is no problem. The problem for the busy Western mind lies in its very simplicity.

He had planned to leave the library at 6.15 precisely but so deep had been his thoughts of nothingness that it was not until nearly ten minutes to seven that he got up to leave. Slowly, at peace with himself, he took his things and evading whatever night warders were about, made his unauthorised way to the Charles II staircase. He climbed two flights to the bell. Only one light had been left on so the place was not full of light. He stood before the bell with the scaffolding rising around and above it, listening. No sound. He and the bell were quite undisturbed.

He removed the dust-sheet from the bell and hung it over the scaffolding. He opened the bag in which was a rope and a hoist system he had brought. He remembers feeling utterly calm and confident. He climbed up on the scaffolding and attached the hoist above the bell. He came down for the rope and as he did, stared again at the great and silent bell.

He remembers what happened next as clearly as a person remembers those few events in life that matter most: a childhood hurt, a first kiss, a first day in a first job. He *remembers* it.

He took the rope. He tied it to the bell. He climbed up again to thread it through the hoist. He climbed down and took in the slack. He started to pull on the rope. The bell was heavier than he expected, and he strained, but soon it slowly rose. The hoist had a ratchet so he could pause and rest. The scaffold gave somewhat. He pulled more. The scaffold strained and heaved and then the bell was clear, its edges off the marble floor. Rothenstein even remembers the collection of dust that had gathered underneath, whose round, shadowed shape he could see emerging as the bell began to rise. It came up slowly, millimetres slow. He stopped when the scaffold creaked too loud. All this he is sure of. He hung the free end of the rope over the scaffold and leaned forward and gently tapped the bell with his knuckles. He *remembers* doing so. There was a distant, very distant sound. Barely more than a whisper, centuries old. He took the mallet from his bag and raised it to the bell.

And then, slowly and at peace, he began to strike the bell, the first strike vibrating out, and then the sound of the second joining it, and then a third melding into the great booming vibrations that came forth and all around him and down and out into the great darkness of the Museum's rooms. Boom, boom, booms of sound. As the sound drove on he heard in the far distance over the tolling the sound of running footsteps. He remembers that.

Gardner heard it in his room a floor below and quarter of a mile away. Quite clearly. The sound of a great and ancient bell ringing out into the Museum's night. He knew immediately what it was, but not how. He rose from his desk listening. It was the Tibetan bell. He *knew* it.

He, too, remembers. Its sound came booming to him and he turned as if called, as if the tolling demand that he came. There was a terrible urgency in the sound, and he, for all his age, found himself walking fast and then breaking into as much of a run as he could manage. He *remembers* that. Some yards outside his office, as he right turned into Room XII, the sound reached a great vibrating crescendo and then, with each extra running step towards it, it began to fade away. The ringing grew quieter, the sound more distant, as if he was running down receding vales of time. He recalls that as that realisation came, he knew as well that Rothenstein was there ahead of him at the bell. He knew that something was happening which had to do with both of them, and was the result somehow of those strange meetings they had had. He ran on, the sound retreating, the marble staircase only just ahead. On he ran, to the first stair, up the steps, looking up through the gyrating balustrades, the scaffolding above the bell already in view about the murky ceilings high above. The bell no more than feet above but still not quite in sight.

The great vibrations still died away, only their distant echo remained, and he found himself running up the stairs into a profound and awesome silence. He turned the last corner of the stair before the bell and saw the strangest sight that ever he saw in his long career at the Museum.

It took him some moments to realise that it *was* Rothenstein. But there he was, seated on the marble floor, cross-legged. His arms were outstretched and his wrists rested on his knees. His back was straight. He was in some kind of meditative or yogic position. He seemed to be staring at the bell, except that his eyes were shut. At his side was a duffle bag, unopened. Above the bell the scaffolding was undisturbed. The bell was shrouded.

Gardner stared at this sight, wondering where other people were – the night warders who should have heard and should have come. The late library staff. Dammit, *somebody* must have heard.

Rothenstein stood up slowly.

'I heard it ringing,' said Gardner, rather pointlessly. 'I *heard* it.'

'Then it must have rung,' said Rothenstein.

Yet his bag, with its ridiculous contents of hoist and mallet and rope, had never been opened. Rothenstein had never done what he remembered afterwards doing. No one else but the two of them ever after said they had heard the bell. Yet at that moment its sound was still tolling in their ears.

They stood before the bell, a great release about them both and something shared forever bonding them. Rothenstein laughed and said something trite like 'You see, I've always been spoilt. I get what I want. Even the bell ringing!'

Gardner remembered staring at his friend's face and seeing the look of loss he had first seen, decades before, finally gone. Rothenstein was smiling with a freedom he had never known. The shadows of a past were gone.

They told me this, all of it, that night by the bell, and in telling me they lost the need to return again. Gardner retired a few months later. We invite him, and Rothenstein as well to the Christmas party, but neither ever comes.

They did not come tonight. So I approach the sound of the bell alone now and without support. Its tolling is far louder than you could ever imagine it might be, its sound is all around me. But no one else seems to have heard and I am frightened. I do not know why I am beginning to run towards it, nor what I expect to see. But the changes I have been through in recent months are perhaps not so different from what Rothenstein must have suffered. And like him I have often stood by the forgotten bell.

Now, in the sound that demands that I come, I understand the terrible nature of the questions he asked. And I recall with dread what Gardner said when I first asked him about Rothenstein. I remember the words as clearly as I can hear the sound of the bell:

'It is rare in life to be a witness at the moment a man's life is changed.'

And even as I remember that, the sound of the bell has changed. Its tolling is receding, its sound fading back across a vale of time. And though I run even faster down the Museum's great corridors I know that before I ever reach it, the bell will have gone back into a silence before which I may not find the courage to be still.

Yet another short story debut, this time by the young British author of *Red Moon and Black Mountain* and *The Grey Mane of Morning*. Her tale ties in with her novels of legendary times and sheds light on events referred to in her books.

The Coming of the Starborn

Joy Chant

Many centuries ago in Khendiol, when the Cities of Bariphen still stood and the Alnei were new to the Wild Magic, a people lived beyond the eastern sea. They were tall and blackhaired, with eyes green as the sea that battered their homeland, and they were very poor. They lived between steep barren hills and a wild ocean, and their fields were rocky and thin-soiled, yielding poor crops to hard labour. Fish made the chief of their diet; they were plentiful in those fierce seas, though not to be won without danger. They kept goats and sheep in the high stony pastures and in the bogs and sea-marshes, but had no other animals. When they worked in their fields and cut the peats they leaned into the harness themselves, and carried their laden baskets home. Few trees grew in that land, and they could spare little timber for anything but their boats. Their houses were built of stone and roofed with turf, scantily furnished. Their treasures were wooden bowls, polished horns, and goat-fells.

Their life was bitterly hard, but in two things they were rich: beauty and learning. They were a handsome people, wide-browed and deep-eyed with strong clear features, and their bearing would have been called majestic if any had seen them who knew the word. As for learning, it was their chief prize. The children did not work beside their parents, but studied; there were very few among the people who could not both read and write, and most could write in several styles, and knew words not used in their daily speech. They had many books; on mathematics or the stars, chronicles of the past or books of thought, or records of voyages. Of all these they were immensely proud; proud too of the men and women whose lives were given to maintaining this lore and teaching the children, nor did they see any folly in sparing these few hands from the labour of survival. For this, they said, made the life of mankind, and what use was it only to survive? And chief of all their pride, they had the Laws. These they all made together, when there was need of law-making, for they were always few. So too they governed their lives, women and men sharing labour and honour equally. Yet there was one family foremost among them, whose lives were all given up to study and interpretation of the Law. The head of that house could not truly be called their ruler; but he or she took the lead in worship, presided over gatherings and spoke first in debate, so might justly be called their king. That indeed was the name given them by some, and by all strangers: but their true title was the Judge, that is, Kiron.

Their histories told of few deeds more exciting than those of daring sailors, for these, and great judges, were their heroes: the courage of their lives was not that of warriors, but they had need enough of it at times. Such a time came, a bad time, as bad as any in the records. A foul winter began with storms that brought the sea up to drown many of their fields, and when the great winds ceased still the salt water stood there, held by the barriers that had not kept it out. Snow thinned their flocks, and the terrible rains that followed it; and a bitter spring brought no relief. Frost continued long, shortening the growing season, nor would those fields the sea had flooded bear at all that year. They had little fuel, and less food to cook over it. Each day more of the old and the less hardy remained huddled under their blankets, and fewer of the weakened people went out to hack at the frozen fields. Then, bitterest of blows, the fish failed them. Whether this was due to the storms or another cause there was no knowing, only that the haggard men sailed farther and farther, and still brought home poor catches. Many of them died. And yet there were more children among them than there had ever been. They had never been more than a thousand in number, often not so many, but now they could foresee the day when there would be twelve hundred of them, or more: four to eat what three ate now.

On rocky islands near their shores were colonies of breeding seals, and but for that many more would have died. That was a harsh choice for them. They hunted the seals, in other seasons, at sea, and partly for that reason were reluctant to kill them now;

also they held them in some reverence and much affection. It was a bitter day and an unhappy gathering when they agreed on that slaughter, and the men who went to execute it were as sick with grief and shame as they were with hunger. Many feared that such a deed would lose them the sea's blessings, and their luck as fishermen and sailors. Of all the deputies of Naracan God of Gods, none was so great as the High Lord Emngar, and the seals were the dearest of his creatures. Some would not go at all, nor eat of the meat so desperately got.

But though the food lay heavy in their stomachs, it nourished them, and what stores were left fed those who could not bear it. Slowly the famine eased. Still-births and losses among the lambs and kids gave a little meat, and their bereaved mothers gave milk. Deaths grew fewer as the cold lessened; the pastures greened, and the flocks fattened. Summer came; but beyond summer and autumn lay another winter, another starving spring, and Kiron debated with the Council whether there was any way to fend off more such times.

On an evening near midsummer the people gathered in Assembly on the hillside above their town. They met in a hollow filled with the sunset, standing or sitting on the ground, and Kiron sat before them on a carved stone, the ancient Judge's Seat, with his daughter beside him. This was the question he put to them; whether they wished to cross the mountains that marked their border, and to strive to increase their lands by taking the valleys beyond. Yet if they succeeded, they would be dispossessing those almost as poor as themselves.

Such a thing had never been mooted before; when they tried to talk of it, the words felt strange on their tongues, and they avoided each others' eyes. For a while they tried to argue it, but when Kiron's nephew, a man named Horenen, said, 'We wept over the seals, and are we to think of killing men? Better for us to starve as honest men than live as brigands,' there was not a voice raised except in assent.

Still, it was hard to starve; and they talked on, seeking other solutions, and finding none. When talk was done they still sat, listening to the harpers as sunlight faded. Most likely it was melancholy, a greater need than usual for company and the comfort of old songs, but however it came about, the sun had set and still they remained, in the dusk and the brightening star-light. There was no moon.

And then across the hillside came nine strangers, and they shimmered with light. Light moved with them, and they trod upon it, a soft radiance like starlight. The harper fell silent; Kiron stood. The strangers came down into the hollow, and through the crowd. There were eight women, and one man. They were clothed like the people, and in height and feature were not unlike them: but they were so beautiful that many who looked at them hid their eyes.

When they stood before Kiron the young man said, 'I greet you, Kiron, and I greet your daughter, and all your people. I am Alunyueth the Prince, and these are my sisters. We come to you sent by the High Lords; we are the Children of Tinoithë.'

Kiron said, 'You are welcome for your own sakes and for the sake of those in whose name you come. Few strangers come here, nor do we go much over the mountains; so pardon us, that we do not know of your father here.'

At that the maidens laughed, and one of them, she who was a little taller than her sisters, a little more splendid even than they, said, 'Indeed you know him, and have seen him often, although his name is strange to you. We have come farther and along a stranger path to find you than you know. Look now!'

She turned, and all her sisters with her, and they lifted their arms to that part of the twilight sky where brightening hung the Silver Branch. There was a deep strangeness in the way they moved, all together, and a strangeness in the very gesture. Their brother said, 'Do you see the fairest of all that fair host, the green and burning one, outshining all? That is Tinoithë. We are Starborn, Kiron.'

The sound from the people was breaths more than voices, and quickly hushed. Kiron was silent, looking where the maidens pointed, and he was glad to feel his daughter's arm against his own. After a moment he answered, 'Could we think you were mortal, and still call ourselves so?'

Alunyueth began to speak. He told how the High Lords had long looked with favour on the people, how they held them in high honour, and how in particular they had been pleased to see how well they bore their recent hardship. Some looked ashamed at that, thinking of the seals, and others wept, remembering their dead. As he spoke the night drew down, and the star-maidens' soft brilliance grew stronger; but the splendour of Alunyueth was such that Kiron's daughter Garinna, though a young woman of great self-command, could neither look at him nor away. He told how the High Lords had found no other place where wisdom was so valued, nowhere else a whole people who made virtue their one goal and their daily habit. 'Who when they see starvation before them will say as Lord Horenon said, "Let us starve like honest men."'

At that there was a murmuring, that he should know Horenon's name and what he said, and also that he called him Lord; for they used no such titles. Horenon looked confused and a little red, until the foremost of the sisters, she who had spoken, turned her head and smiled at him. Then he grew very pale.

Such praise could only be a pleasure to them; yet it was one so strange that they grew uneasy at it, and Kiron begged Aluny-ueth to say no more.

'Courteous guest, praise is sweet, and sweets are best when tasted sparingly. Yet why should we be commended? We have done no more than we ought. Honour may be lost by too much thought of it.'

'Oh, but there is more to be said!' cried the maidens, and there was never heard such a chiming of voices. 'Indeed,' said their leader, 'we were not sent here only to praise you, and what my brother has said is no more than explanation for what he has yet to say. You may find the commendation of the High Lords more sharp than sweet, before all is done.'

'Aiië Nath speaks truth; it is their way to lay great burdens on those who please them. Have you not already found it so? So you may again. So may we: this figure of the dance that we share with you may teach us grief. Not everything is yet revealed to us. But all are under command, in the heavens as here, and we must step as the music bids us. Hear me, then.

'This people has been chosen for a task and a destiny; and if you will accept it you must do so knowing that in ages to come your descendants may regret the quiet of such a life as this you lead, with all its hardship. What that task is has not been told us;

if it is, we will tell you. But we know that you who are few shall be many, a people renowned and mighty, and that the blood of the stars shall be mingled with yours, if you will have it so. Therefore are we sent to you, and therefore make our request: that my sisters shall find here husbands, and I a wife. And for my bride I ask your daughter Garinna.'

Now the Judge's elder child, his son, had been drowned some years before, and Garinna was his heir. Because of that her father's consent was needed for her marriage, though other women of full age were subject to no one in such matters. So though her soul seemed to flower out through her skin Garinna kept a calm face, while Kiron looked at her and said, 'I doubt if you expected to be courted so publicly, child. Well, I expected to know your sweetheart's father better than by sight only. This is a strange thing, to marry among strangers; but these seem well spoken for, and to come of a decent family.'

Alunyueth laughed, and the Princess, who had thought his voice even more beautiful than his face, found his laugh best of all. But she kept her eyes on her father and said steadily, 'This is not something to be decided by the three of us, nor perhaps so quickly; for if I have understood the Prince, to grant his asking will be to accept the task the High Lords give us, whatever that may be. That needs the consent of us all.'

'You remind me well,' said Kiron. Then he put the question to the people, whether the strangers' request should be granted; and they cried loudly and all together that it should. Then Alunyueth turned smiling to Garinna, and said, 'It needs but your word now, lady. Will you give me your hand?'

And she, who had ever been grave and cool, ruled always by thought, whose peace had never yet been broken by man or boy, knew that her calm was gone forever, and did not regret it. 'My hand and my heart, and my faith through life,' she said, and she went without hesitation to his side, taking the hand he held out. He said softly, 'Will you do so, beloved, though as my sister has said, it is only a certain measure of the Dance we may remain? In twenty of your years, or a little less, we must take our place in it again.'

She heard the words; but the sound of that 'beloved' half drowned their meaning, and she answered smiling, 'If I may

share twenty years with you, I am fortunate beyond dreams.'
She did not offend modesty by her boldness, for that was not
much valued among them; but the passion that was born in her,
that she did not seek to hide, proved as perilous as such passion
can.

Then the sisters told their names: Keranomoië, Havonil,
Issumathë, Halamenithë, Nidavathil, Rulanemissë, Kerutu-
vayë, and Aiië Nath, most beautiful of all. She said at once, 'I
dare not be patient, lest another forestall me and win the heart of
him I love; for if the Lord Horenon will have me, my choice is
made.'

So it was; and since she had no family house from which he
might fetch her, she went with Horenon that night to his home.
Nor were her sisters long unwed. Four of the Council, a scholar,
two farmers, and a shipwright, were still unmarried, and were
chosen by the Starborn; a famed sailor married Halamenithë, a
house-builder Issumathë, and Nidavathil married a shepherd
lad, the youngest of the grooms. All told their husbands, as their
brother had his wife, of the limit set to their time together; and
perhaps amid the bridal gaiety some of the men heeded those
words as little as had Garinna. For although Alunyueth had
spoken of less than twenty years, she called it twenty and
stretched it in her mind; and twenty years ahead seem long
enough, to a young woman.

Alunyueth was henceforth of Kiron's family and acknow-
ledged co-heir with Garinna, and he devoted himself to studying
the Laws. Few of the people encountered him daily, or at shared
tasks, and to most he remained always the Prince. With the
daughters of Tinoithë it was not the same. The skills they set
themselves to learn were commoner ones, of field and house,
and the families who taught them, the neighbours who laughed
with them at their errors and showed them better ways, soon lost
their awe of them. They called them the Brides, and saw them
too often as women dismayed at a failed batch of bread or
struggling with a reluctant milch-goat to think of them long as
Daughters of the Stars. Indeed, they regarded them as gay and
clumsy girls long after they were skilful housewives. The sisters
dressed as the other women did, scarfed up their hair for work
like them, grew dishevelled beside them and red-handed at the

fish cleaning, and either their strange light dimmed or the people ceased to see it. But their unearthly beauty never lessened; and when at festivals they stood out to dance together, in a pattern not learned on earth, then they were the Starborn again.

Only their husbands never forgot they were not mortal. Only they saw how strange, how difficult and fascinating, the Starborn found the mortal world: how hard it was for them to live in the human rhythm of days and nights, meals and work and sleep. They knew that the Children of Tinoithë found flesh as strange a garment as the shifts and shawls with which they covered it, were as astonished by its delights as by its weaknesses and indignities; they could not forget that their brides were strangers to the earth. Only they and Garinna knew how often they woke alone at night, while the Starborn walked together under the stars, escaping briefly from the trammels of humanity. And none but those nine couples could guess the pain there could be in loving across so deep a gulf.

The sons came first; Emneron, the child of Alunyueth and Garinna, within a year of their marriage, and over the next three years his sisters' sons. All remembered then that the Brides were not women born of women; being with child was very strange to them, a bondage to the flesh indeed, and some of them found it hard. They knew less than any mortal girl with her first child could; it was impossible not to pity them, not to be moved as seeing how terror mingled with their love for their children. But they forgot all distress in marvelling to watch the babies grow, and those near to them hardly knew whether to be more astonished at the Starborn's wonder, or their own lack of it. All the nine found the effects of time a constant amazement and delight – every year a different spring, an autumn unlike the last – and in the growth of their children this reached its furthest pitch. Alunyueth said to his wife, 'My life has already been longer than you can imagine, and will be longer than your words can tell; yet all those ages have fewer memories than four years here. We have only one life, the same life, always; but mortals live so many. I was never a child; I shall never be old. Only what I am, always. Do you find us dull, being so unchanging?'

She could only look at him and laugh amazed. When she saw how time passed him by, and by his sisters, she dreaded the fading of her own beauty, feared he would find the effect of years less magical in her than in Emneron; yet Alunyueth said, 'In loving a mortal it seems I love many women! You are always becoming new to me. I dare not look away, for fear of missing something of you entirely.'

All things went well in those years. Land and sea yielded the people more abundance than ever before, winters were mild and summers sweet. Seven years after Emneron's birth the old king died, and Garinna succeeded him. Alunyueth shared her throne; indeed it was he and not she who was called Kiron, though until then that title had been borne by men and women alike. The Prince bestowed another on his wife; Tayissa he called her, and said that so should the wife of his heir always be named. That is the only star-name that was ever given openly to a mortal. In these days it is commonly spoken as Tayis, and said to mean Great Queen; but what its true meaning may be, if it has one, is not known.

The eldest of the Starborn's daughters was An'gelinna, born to Aiië Nath when Emneron, who was to be her husband, was six years old. Within two years all her sisters had borne girls, and Nidavathil gave birth to twins. But Garinna had no second child. The children of Tinoithë became teachers to their children as they grew, and they learned star-lore from the first. That was the first time a difference showed between them and other children, for they did not weary as others did. They could spend all day at school and play, and half the night learning other lessons, and never seem tired. Though they were of the people in all ways, and played with their neighbours' children, they came to seek each others' company more as they grew older. For their minds began to outdistance those of their mortal friends even as their beauty outmatched theirs.

So Time and the Dance went on: and the day came, when Emneron was nearing his eighteenth birthday, that Alunyueth took his wife's hands and said, 'Alas, beloved, the time has come; and the Great Dance claims me.'

Then Garinna forgot her station, and her years, and her wisdom, and all but her love for her husband; and she wept and clung to him and implored him to stay a little longer, a season, a month. 'It cannot be,' he said. 'There are measures in the

Dance; we must return to it.' But she begged for a little grace, for time to take leave, not that he should go then. 'Even four days would be too long,' he said. 'Would you have me break my purpose, only for days?'

'For anything,' she said. 'Three days, two, one: anything, so it is not now!'

So he yielded, because of his own great love and grief, and stayed two nights longer. So may even the highest fail in wisdom at times. For their love, ever strong, had never burned so fierce before; and Garinna conceived her daughter, last of the Starborn.

Over all the years the Children of Tinoithë had not aged, and when they gathered to depart, in the hollow where they had first come, it seemed to their husbands and to Garinna that no time at all had passed since they came treading on light to the Assembly. Even Horenon wept; but their eyes were clear. Then Aiië Nath said, 'Do not blame us that we cannot weep, but pity us. For you are mortal, and time brings change to you, and the worst of your griefs has end. But we may neither change nor forget. When the earth itself is forgotten, we shall be remembering you, and grieving.'

Sad was the parting. Yet the Starborn children shed no more tears than their immortal parents, since for them the parting was not complete.

Then Garinna ruled alone and ruled well; and in time, when her daughter was born, she found there was sweetness still in life. It was well for her that there was little leisure to feel all her grief. Time closed behind the Children of Tinoithë. It seemed soon that only their lovers felt their absence daily, and knew their loss as a living pain, very soon that there were children growing up who had to be told of them, and heard the telling like any other tale of the past. One of them was Starborn herself.

The prosperous years went on, and the Children of the Stars grew; and as their years increased so did the life that they shared with none of their mortal comrades, only with each other and the stars. Each year left them strengthened in knowledge and skill, in closer communion with their immortal kindred. They were the first mortals to cross the Border, the first of the Twin-Souled: in them was the Star Magic begun.

Perhaps it was because they lived a divided life that they seemed to live more slowly than those of unmixed blood. They were comrades still, youths and maidens, at an age when others would have been lovers. Even when they did come to love and made their choices, they did not marry soon, and they married only among themselves. Emneron was thirty-six and An'gelinna thirty when they wed, and they were the first. Then the Queen gave up her throne to her son, and he was Kiron, and An'gelinna Tayissa.

A time came when hunger was once more a shadow on their future. No blight had come; the land brought forth as abundantly as ever it could, but less abundantly than the people. The increase they had long ago foreseen had come, but the land grew no richer, and they began to be straitened. Yet it bred in them not foreboding but restlessness, and now when they talked of what might be done, they expected to find an answer. When Emneron called an Assembly, saying that he had news to tell, they gathered to hear it eagerly. The King was in that year forty-three years old, and it was a wonder to all that the glory of his youth, that had begun to flower twenty years before, still bloomed freshly: but so it was with all the Starborn.

Emneron said, 'We grow too many for our ancient land to bear; the time has come for some or all to leave it. I have strange tidings for you. A command has been given to me and to my cousins, that we stay here no longer. We are to look for the swans, and to follow where they lead us, we and our children, and all who choose to come with us. We are to be shown a new land to live in, a land more spacious and fertile than this, and that shall in time surely become as dear to us; or to our children. Nor is that all we shall find there; but more we do not yet know. We, the Children of the Stars, must go; all others are free to choose. Yet, my kinfolk and friends, I would not have us divided. The destiny my father foretold was for all the people. All must take their own counsel, and it is true I cannot believe that the first years in this new land will be easy, nor that peace and plenty will come soon. But I ask you to come with me.'

This was a thing undreamed of, and they were slow to speak, because of its strangeness, and because they loved their comfortless home. But they loved Emneron also, and had faith in him;

and the destiny assented to so long ago could not now be refused. The debate could lead to only one end, that they resolved every one to follow the swans with the Starborn. Only the King's mother Garinna, though she did not speak against it, wept and was loth to go. 'For here,' she said, 'I was Alunyueth's bride.'

Emneron went soon over the mountains, into the country of their neighbours, and offered them the inheritance of the land and all that was in it, houses and flocks and goods and the crops in the ground, all that the people could not take. They were amazed, for their only dealings across the mountains until then had been raiding over the border. They swore friendship to Kiron and his people for ever, and granted gladly what he asked of them – timber, of which that land had abundance, for the building of ships. They gave it and helped convey it, and some stayed to learn something of ships and the sea, for they were ignorant in those matters, having no coasts.

So for two years the people built ships and waited. In that time Garinna the wife of Alunyueth (for she was not a widow) died, and after all never left those shores.

In the spring when Emneron was forty-five years old, the swans came: the great sea-swans, white as foam, whose wings spread twice the height of a man, birds never seen before in those waters and but rarely by sailors. They rode the harbour in a great flock, while the people stowed into the ships all they had prepared, and led aboard the animals they meant to take. Those of their neighbours who were there to see them go vowed again their lasting friendship; and it may be said here that those vows have been kept, and that there in Vala the tomb of Garinna is cared for to this day. Then Emneron and his people pulled in their anchors and departed from the home of their forefathers, sailing with the swans flying before them; and there were few who did not weep.

When they had been some days at sea they came to an island. Kiron said that it was not the land they sought, but in a bay there the swans rested, and they all disembarked. It was a gentle shore, silver-sanded, and around the harbour on smooth green lawns were houses of grey stone; but they saw no people. An old man came to greet them, white-haired but not past strength, and he spoke to them in their own tongue. 'Rest here, and replenish your stores; all is prepared for you.' Emneron thanked him and asked where were the people of that hospitable land; and the old man answered, 'Here I am.'

'Do you live here alone?' asked the King: and their host replied, 'At times I do.'

The quiet of that island land was wonderful; even its strangeness yielded to it, so that the voyagers rested there in perfect ease. After a few days the Warden (so the old man had bidden them call him) returned, and led the Starborn away. He took them to a hill near the southern coast, green and bare, the highest point of the island. From there they could see all of it save the northern shores. And all around them moved the shimmering sea, white-veined, grey and brown and green, a warmer colour where the sun lit it around the beaches, melting in the distance into the silvery brightness of the sky. They stood about the old man, looking where he looked, west into the shining haze.

'There lies your land,' he said. 'Hidden in light: though you will find darkness enough there when you first come to it. Do not think it is given you as an inheritance only, a gift of heaven. It is given you as a charge; you are to be its guardians. It has need of them. It will not be a peaceful possession for many years, nor always remain so when it is won. It is not as other lands of the world; it is on the Border. Long ago when the stars were new a High Lord had his throne there; but those days ended. It was long empty. But now, evil powers have hold of it. You are to drive them out, and keep them out; your task is not simply to take the land for yourselves, but to keep it from others. Not from your fellow men, only from such as these. They will not yield it lightly, nor ever cease trying to return, for it is the property of that land that any power wielded there increases in strength, as theirs now does, and as yours will. Therefore the High Lords intend that a power for good shall hold it, and not these, that grow ever mightier in evil and soon will stretch out to harm those who live ignorant of danger beyond their borders. It is for that they put the blood of the Stars into you, for that they have given the Star Magic into your hands. This is your destiny; to take and cleanse and defend that land, and never to abandon it, until Naracan himself free you: lest he who had his throne there once, set it there again.'

They were silent a while, until Emneron said, 'My people are not warriors; or not yet. No more am I.'

'But you are an Enchanter, as are your kindred here. It is for you to keep your people safe, while they grow strong and learn their task. Have no doubt of yourselves; the work is within your strength, or you would not have been given it.'

An'gelinna's brother Argerth said, 'So our power is bound to the land itself. May it not be used elsewhere? And are we forbidden to leave the land?'

'Much of such knowledge you must discover for yourself; but I believe that outside those borders you will find your power weakened, maybe lost altogether. As for leaving – it is not forbidden, you are not prisoners, and your mortal kindred may do so if they wish. But the land must not be left undefended; and the Starborn ought never to leave it without great cause. Trust is placed in you, though you are free to make what choices you will.

'The Starborn should not leave, that is, until they come here; but here is a command for you and for all who come after, that each at your own appointed time you come here to this island to end your days. Those who die untimely must be brought here for burial. All the Starborn; those who are not Enchanters as well as those who are. Nor only those who live and die with honour.' He saw their startled looks, and shook his head. 'Some will not, never doubt it. There will be enemies among you as well as without.' One of them said, 'Because we are half mortal, and therefore corruptible?'

'No,' he said sharply, 'because you are not Naracan! Do not think the Immortals cannot err. It is not only men you go to fight. I tell you, your mortal part is your safer! What raises you above it, puts you in worse peril of a fall; your immortal blood is both your strength and your weakness.

'And here is another warning; or you may call it a prophecy. You are mortal and subject to time, and therefore even the Star Magic will suffer change. In your future I see three dark times; yet from each you may emerge stronger, so long as you keep faith and do not despair. Beware of despair; it is as dangerous an

enemy as that vanished lord whom the land remembers. Only
with the fourth change comes the end; but whether that will be a
fall or a rising, I cannot see. It is very far off. Tell your heirs of
this, the warning is for them, for these things are in the future,
and you shall not see even the first of the changes.

'One more command, and I have done. You are the founders
of the Nine Houses of the Starborn, and as you have wed, so
must all who come after you. This is a hard command; that all
the Children of the Stars shall make their marriages within the
kindred, or lose their power and forfeit it for their heirs. The
service of the Magic is hard enough for those who inherit half
their being from the stars; those of more mortality could not
bear it. Even those who are not Twin-Souled, and there will be
many at times, must obey this for the sake of their children.
Only your house, Emneron, is free of this bidding, because the
Children of Alunyueth are unlike the other Houses in this, that
their power shall never diminish so long as the Star Magic
endures.'

'We have heard; we will remember,' said Emneron. His face
was grave, and so were they all, but when he looked round at his
kindred he smiled. 'This is no light charge we are given; but let
us not be daunted. Come, brothers and sisters, who will swear
an oath with me? Let us pledge ourselves to the defence of this
new land of ours against every enemy, mortal or immortal, to
the utmost of our strength, until our charge is taken from us.
Let us promise that it shall be conquered once, and then never
again!'

So they swore; and so do all the Star Enchanters to this day.
The Warden said, 'That is well done. Now come.' He led them
down, back to the harbour and to his own house there; and then
to eight of the nine Houses he gave those things which are called
their Treasures. But the Treasure of Kiron's own house he did
not hold in trust, and it did not come into their possession then;
and the tale of it is told elsewhere.

After that the Starborn returned to the rest of the people, and
they waited with them until the morning when they woke to hear
the swans calling from the harbour. Then they took leave of the
Warden and went into the ships again, and the swans rose
among the sails and beat away before them. Many days longer

they voyaged, led by the swans, till at last they came to the ocean's western shore and the place of their destiny. They sailed into harbour where H'ara Tunij now stands, and there they beached their ships. And thus did the people now known as the Harani come to the land they first called Herathun, the Swans' Shore; but that after, in another tongue, came to be better named – Kedrinh, the Starlit Land.

And it was as the Warden had said; the power of the Starborn increased in that land, so that behind the defences of their enchantments the people lived a while in safety, planting new and richer fields and reaping their first harvests, building a place they could defend, and learning the use of weapons. The great deeds of those days belonged to the Starborn, and there were many of them, as those eighteen strove to keep more than a thousand safe: deeds like that which gained Emneron his nickname of The White, when ambushed and alone he fought a great duel of power that left him silver-haired before he was fifty. There were terrible enemies faced, and not all the cousins went back living to the Island. The time of the mortal heroes came later, when they went out to begin the scouring of their land. That was the beginning of their long history, and of the war that has never ended.

As all Vandarei knows, they won the whole land for themselves in time, from the Northern River to the Southern Sea, and the hosts of evil were driven into the wastes of the far north: but it was not in the time of that first generation, nor of their children. Many years passed before the kingdoms were established and the Nine Fair Cities built. It was not Emneron the White but his great-great-grandson, the second Emneron, who saw the realm made safe, and his son for whom the Crown of Stars was forged. Then began the long glory of the Silver Age; but those days were far in the future and many bitter struggles away, when the little nation of farmers and fishermen with their small band of protectors raised that first wall of white stones beside their harbour. That wall still stands. Only one marvel of Kedrinh is as old as those oldest days, and that is it. There she stands to this day, grown and glorified, but at her heart the city that Emneron founded: the Pearl of the North, built of white stone above the sea, first and fairest of the Nine. Kirontin they called her then, the Judgment Place; but the name she now bears is known to all the world. There in the shining hall the banners hang, the Emerald is worn, the Children of the Stars gather while the Holly Captain keeps the door: there the Harani, mortal and half-mortal, make again their unbroken vow. So it has been for twice a thousand years, and so may it be, for many more.

J. G. Ballard is now unanimously recognised as one of the major British contemporary authors. His science fiction usually takes place in 'inner space' and outerspace excursions are rare in his oeuvre. The following story is a rare exception and, furthermore, is also pure fantasy in a cosmological vein pioneered by Jorge Luis Borges and Italo Calvino. Ballard's last books have been *Hello America* and *Myths of the Near Future*.

Report on an Unidentified Space Station

J. G. Ballard

Survey Report 1

By good luck we have been able to make an emergency landing on this uninhabited space station. There have been no casualties. We all count ourselves fortunate to have found safe haven at a moment when the expedition was clearly set on disaster.

The station carries no identification markings and is too small to appear on our charts. Although of elderly construction it is soundly designed and in good working order, and seems to have been used in recent times as a transit depot for travellers resting at mid-point in their journeys. Its interior consists of a series of open passenger concourses, with comfortably equipped lounges and waiting rooms. As yet we have not been able to locate the bridge or control centre. We assume that the station was one of many satellite drogues surrounding a larger command unit, and was abandoned when a decline in traffic left it surplus to the needs of the parent transit system.

A curious feature of the station is its powerful gravitational field, far stronger than would be suggested by its small mass. However, this probably represents a faulty reading by our instruments. We hope shortly to complete our repairs and are grateful to have found shelter on this relic of the now forgotten migrations of the past.

Estimated diameter of the station: 500 metres.

Survey Report 2

Our repairs are taking longer than we first estimated. Certain pieces of equipment will have to be reconstructed from scratch, and to shorten this task we are carrying out a search of our temporary home.

To our surprise we find that the station is far larger than we guessed. A thin local atmosphere surrounds the station, composed of interstellar dust attracted by its unusually high gravity. This fine vapour obscured the substantial bulk of the station and led us to assume that it was no more than a few hundred metres in diameter.

We began by setting out across the central passenger concourse that separates the two hemispheres of the station. This wide deck is furnished with thousands of tables and chairs. But on reaching the high partition doors 200 metres away we discovered that the restaurant deck is only a modest annexe to a far larger concourse. An immense roof three storeys high extends across an open expanse of lounges and promenades. We explored several of the imposing staircases, each equipped with a substantial mezzanine, and found that they lead to identical concourses above and below.

The space station has clearly been used as a vast transit facility, comfortably accommodating many thousands of passengers. There are no crew quarters or crowd control posts. The absence of even a single cabin indicates that this army of passengers spent only a brief time here before being moved on, and must have been remarkably self-disciplined or under powerful restraint.

Estimated diameter: 1 mile.

Survey Report 3

A period of growing confusion. Two of our number set out 48 hours ago to explore the lower decks of the station, and have so far failed to return. We have carried out an extensive search and fear that a tragic accident has taken place. None of the hundreds of elevators is in working order, but our companions may have entered an unanchored cabin and fallen to their deaths. We managed to force open one of the heavy doors and gazed with awe down the immense shaft. Many of the elevators within the station could comfortably carry a thousand passengers. We hurled several pieces of furniture down the shaft, hoping to time the interval before their impact, but not a sound returned to us. Our voices echoed away into a bottomless pit.

Perhaps our companions are marooned far from us on the lower levels? Given the likely size of the station, the hope remains that a maintenance staff occupies the crew quarters on some remote upper deck, unaware of our presence here. As soon as we contact them they will help us to rescue our companions.

Estimated diameter: 10 miles.

Survey Report 4

Once again our estimate of the station's size has been substantially revised. The station clearly has the dimensions of a large asteroid or even a small planet. Our instruments indicate that there are thousands of decks, each extending for miles across an undifferentiated terrain of passenger concourses, lounge and restaurant terraces. As before there is no sign of any crew or supervisory staff. Yet somehow a vast passenger complement was moved through this planetary waiting room.

While resting in the armchairs beneath the unvarying light we have all noticed how our sense of direction soon vanishes. Each of us sits at a point in space that at the same time seems to have no precise location but could be anywhere within these endless vistas of tables and armchairs. We can only assume that the passengers moving along these decks possessed some instinctive homing device, a mental model of the station that allowed them to make their way within it.

In order to establish the exact dimensions of the station and, if possible, rescue our companions we have decided to abandon our repair work and set out on an unlimited survey, however far this may take us.

Estimated diameter: 500 miles.

Survey Report 5

No trace of our companions. The silent interior spaces of the station have begun to affect our sense of time. We have been travelling in a straight line across one of the central decks for what seems an unaccountable period. The same pedestrian concourses, the same mezzanines attached to the stairways, and the same passenger lounges stretch for miles under an unchanging light. The energy needed to maintain this degree of illumination suggests that the operators of the station were used to a full passenger complement. However, there are unmistakable signs that no one has been here since the remote past. Clearly, whoever designed the station based the transit systems within it on a timetable of gigantic dimensions.

We press on, following the same aisle that separates two adjacent lounge concourses. We rest briefly at fixed intervals, but despite our steady passage we sense that we are not moving at all, and may well be trapped within a small waiting room whose apparently infinite dimensions we circle like ants on a sphere. Paradoxically, our instruments confirm that we are penetrating a structure of rapidly increasing mass.

Is the entire universe no more than an infinitely vast space terminal?

Estimated diameter: 5,000 miles.

Survey Report 6

We have just made a remarkable discovery! Our instruments have detected that a slight but perceptible curvature is built into the floors of the station. The ceilings recede behind us and dip fractionally towards the decks below, while the disappearing floors form a distinct horizon.

So the station is a curvilinear structure of finite form! There must be meridians that mark out its contours, and an equator that will return us to our original starting point. We all feel an immediate surge of hope. Already we may have stumbled on an equatorial line, and despite the huge length of our journey we may in fact be going home.

Estimated diameter: 50,000 miles.

Survey Report 7

Our hopes have proved to be short-lived. Excited by the thought that we had mastered the station, and cast a net around its invisible bulk, we were pressing on with renewed confidence. However, we now know that although these curvatures exist, they extend in all directions. Each of the walls curves away from its neighbours, the floors from the ceilings. The station, in fact, is an expanding structure whose size appears to increase exponentially. The longer the journey undertaken by a passenger, the greater the incremental distance he will have to travel. The virtually un-limited facilities of the station suggest that its passengers were embarked on extremely long, if not infinite, journeys.

Needless to say, the complex architecture of the station has ominous implications for us. We realise that the size of the station is a measure, not of the number of passengers embarked – though this must have been vast – but of the length of the journeys that must be undertaken within it. Indeed, there should ideally be only one passenger. A solitary voyager embarked on an infinite journey would require an infinity of transit lounges. As there are, fortunately, more than one of us we can assume that the station is a finite structure with the appearance of an infinite one. The degree to which it approaches an infinite size is merely a measure of the will and ambition of its passengers.

Estimated diameter: 1 million miles.

Survey Report 8

Just when our spirits were at their lowest ebb we have made a small but significant finding. We were moving across one of the limitless passenger decks, a prey to all fears and speculations, when we noticed the signs of recent habitation. A party of travellers has paused here in the recent past. The chairs in the central concourse have been disturbed, an elevator door has been forced, and there are the unmistakable traces left by weary voyagers. Without doubt there were more than two of them, so we must regretfully exclude our lost companions.

But there are others in the station, perhaps embarked on a journey as endless as our own!

We have also noticed slight variations in the decor of the station, in the design of light fittings and floor tiles. These may seem trivial, but multiplying them by the virtually infinite size of the station we can envisage a gradual evolution in its architecture. Somewhere in the station there may well be populated enclaves, even entire cities, surrounded by empty passenger decks that stretch on forever like free space. Perhaps there are nation-states whose civilisations rose and declined as their peoples paused in their endless migrations across the station.

Where were they going? And what force propelled them on their meaningless journeys? We can only hope that they were driven forward by the greatest of all instincts, the need to establish the station's size.

Estimated diameter: 5 light years.

Survey Report 9

We are jubilant! A growing euphoria has come over us as we move across these great concourses. We have seen no further trace of our fellow passengers, and it now seems likely that we were following one of the inbuilt curvatures of the station and had crossed our own tracks.

But this small setback counts for nothing now. We have accepted the limitless size of the station, and this awareness fills us with feelings that are almost religious. Our instruments confirm what we have long suspected, that the empty space across which we travelled from our own solar system in fact lies within the interior of the station, one of the many vast lacunae set in its endlessly curving walls. Our solar system and its planets, the millions of other solar systems that constitute our galaxy, and the island universes themselves all lie within the boundaries of the station. The station is coeval with the cosmos, and constitutes the cosmos. Our duty is to travel across it on a journey whose departure point we have already begun to forget, and whose destination is the station itself, every floor and concourse within it.

So we move on, sustained by our faith in the station, aware that every step we take thereby allows us to reach a small part of that destination. By its existence the station sustains us, and gives our lives their only meaning. We are glad that in return we have begun to worship the station.

Estimated diameter: 15,000 light years.

A young British writer of Welsh lineage, Christopher Evans is the author of two well-received novels: *Capella's Golden Eye* and *The Insider*. His tale shows us the other side of fairy tales.

The Rites of Winter

Christopher Evans

> And fire and ice within me fight
> Beneath the suffocating night.
> > A. E. Housman

There were heavy snows that November, and by the turn of the year Stella's supplies of fuel were running low. She was forced to collect brushwood from the countryside surrounding the village, and celebrated her twenty-second birthday with mild frostbite of the hands. She kept a fire burning in the main room throughout the day, banking it up at night so that a residual warmth and sometimes even an ember remained when she rose the following morning. It was just as well that the inn was empty of guests and she did not have to provide extra fires; it would be difficult enough to survive the winter as it was.

The bleak, bitter weather reflected her inner state of mind. Her husband, Thomas, had died that autumn, a withered, exhausted man who looked twice his thirty-six years. He had expired in her arms without a word, as if he was glad to give up the ghost of his life. Their last guest of the season, a woman called Marguerite, had left the inn the previous day. With her had gone Thomas's last hope of survival. Marguerite: pale and blonde, with a smile that enchanted and blue eyes as deep and ancient as an ocean; she had stolen Thomas away, bewitched him then sucked the life from him.

The doctor who had come reluctantly from the village had told her that a wasting disease had killed him. Stella knew better, for only weeks before her husband had been a vigorous man in the prime of his life and no disease could act so quickly. But she said nothing, aware that the villagers had never liked her or her husband. The inn lay on the outskirts of the village, but it might as well have been on the moon for all the contact they had had with it. When she and Thomas had taken over the inn two years before, the previous owner had warned them that the villagers mistrusted anyone who sheltered travellers bound to or from the city. They believed the city to be a source of evil; its inhabitants possessed demonic powers, they claimed, and could conjure spirits from shadows, invade the minds of others, turn their enemies to ash with their gaze, and much more.

She and Thomas had dismissed these stories as superstition born of drudgery; they had never visited the city, but came from a town in the west where all shades of opinion were tolerated but none blindly accepted. Now Stella regretted their dismissiveness; Marguerite was no ordinary woman but a succubus who thrived by draining the lives of those she seduced.

The doctor had departed saying that he would send someone from the village to bury Thomas. But that night the temperature had dropped sharply and there was a heavy snowstorm. Thomas was lying in the wine cellar where she had found him dying. The tiny window high in its wall had blown open during the night, and the next morning his body was covered with a layer of snow. Stella bolted the window but did not disturb the body; winter had arrived, the earth would soon be frozen, and there would be no burial for her husband until spring.

In the immediate aftermath of his death, Stella wrote a letter to the authorities in the city, telling them what had happened and demanding that Marguerite be tracked down and dispatched as a witch. She trudged through two miles of knee-high snow to post the letter, but on her return had immediately realised the futility of the gesture. Even assuming that the authorities believed her story, she had no evidence that they would act on it; indeed, if such creatures as Marguerite were commonplace in the city, perhaps these very authorities might be numbered among them and would seek to protect their own kind. There was also a more obvious practical difficulty: if the road to the city was impassable with snow, postal deliveries would be suspended until the weather improved.

She spent the dark, chill months huddled around the fire, feeling strangely secure in her solitude. She hardened her mind against thoughts of her dead husband; if she became restless she would wash linen, iron curtains or take a brush to corners of the inn that had not been swept in years. Some nights she would wake to the darkness and the keen wind outside with the fleeting memory of some disturbing dream which faded even as she tried to snatch at it. Then she would remember how Marguerite had mesmerised Thomas from the moment he saw her and had sapped everything vital from him before vanishing.

One morning in March Stella awoke to find the air milder and the frost flowers vanished from her window. The ribbon of road which led north to the city was visible in patches, and snow fell from tree branches. In recent years the weather had become violently capricious; as quickly as winter had come, it had departed. Soon travellers en route to the city would start arriving from the south.

She removed the caged, hooded crow from its winter quarters in a south-facing room and set it on the tall pedestal outside the inn; the bird had been inherited from the previous owner and gave the inn its name. The placing of the crow outside the inn always symbolised the start of a new season, and although she was aware that her responsibilities would be heavy without Thomas, she was determined to carry on alone.

She spent the next few days spring-cleaning the guest rooms. Then, one morning, she was drawn to the window by the fractious cries of the crow and saw a stranger chasing away a small boy from the village who had evidently been throwing snowballs at the bird. When the boy was gone, the stranger turned towards the inn, his long cloak damp at its edges from the melting snow.

He was a good-looking, bearded man little older than herself, with dark hair and brown eyes. He gave his name as Simon and handed her a silver coin. This was enough to pay for one month's board. Most guests usually stayed no more than a few days, but the coin was offered without expectation of change.

'Have you travelled far?' she asked him.

He gave a thin smile and a hint of a nod. 'Far enough.'

She handed him the key to the guest room next to her own; the fire downstairs kept both rooms warmer than the rest. Later, when she brought him some cheese and cold pork, she found that the door to his room was locked.

'Leave it outside,' he called to her.

He stayed in his room all day, and at dinner she left a bowl of thick vegetable soup outside his door. Late that evening, while she was sitting beside the fire darning a skirt, he entered the room.

She nodded to him and he seated himself in the rocking chair opposite her. It was where her husband had always sat in the evenings, drinking wine and regaling their guests with fictitious stories of his exploits as a youth. Simon produced a white clay pipe and a small knife with which he scraped the dottle from the bowl. He kept his tobacco in a leather pouch attached to his belt; its scent was more aromatic than that to which she was accustomed.

Intent on her darning, she asked, 'Are you bound for the city?'

Curlicues of smoke shrouded his head. 'Not at present. Do you live alone here?'

'Yes. My husband died last autumn.'

He made no reply to this. Stella snipped the woollen thread and inspected the patch. 'He's lying in the cellar. The ground froze before he could be buried.'

Logs collapsed in the fireplace with a cascade of sparks which were sucked up the dark chimney.

'Are you travelling on business?'

'Of a sort.' He began to rock gently in the chair. 'It must be hard to be here alone.'

Stella rose, laying the skirt over the back of a chair. 'The inn has been empty all winter. My only concern has been to keep myself fed and warm.'

As if to emphasise this she knelt and added more logs to the fire. But it was not entirely true. She had been lonely.

The logs quickly took fire. She saw his image reflected in the curved brass of the coal scuttle.

'You'll be needing more wood,' he said.

'I'll be hoping for a delivery of coal as soon as the road is clear.'

'Ah.'

As she rose from the hearth, so did he from his chair.

'Well, goodnight,' he said.

When she heard his door close, she crept upstairs and entered her own room. She knelt at the spy-hole which she and her husband had discovered soon after taking over the inn; the previous owner had evidently been something of a voyeur. She herself wanted to be sure that this man who called himself Simon was just that: a man. She had been chastened by her encounter with Marguerite.

When he finally began to undress, she had already imagined that he might reveal a body covered with scales or strange growths. But there was nothing: just a leanly muscular frame, with a line of dark hair running down the centre of his belly to the denser hair at his groin.

He withdrew a book from his satchel, got into bed and began to read by candlelight. She waited. He was facing her and once, when he looked up from his reading and stared in her direction, she had the uncanny impression that he knew she was there. But the spy-hole was well concealed and he could not have been aware of her scrutiny. Soon afterwards he snuffed out the candle and all was dark.

When Stella rose the next morning she found she had neglected to lock her bedroom door. Simon had already risen and she saw him dragging a fallen birch trunk from a nearby copse into the back yard. She watched from the window as he went to the woodshed and returned with an axe before stripping down to his undershirt.

The axe flashed in the wintry sunlight and the blade bit into the wood. He worked steadily and methodically, tossing the logs into a pile against the wall. Stella went downstairs and took the crow outside. It immediately began to emit its harsh *kraa* sounds. Normally she imagined that the bird was soliciting guests when it crowed, but on this occasion its cries seemed less welcoming than admonitory.

The fire was already ablaze in the hearth. She put on water to heat for his bath. When he came inside she asked him if he wanted the water brought to his room.

'As you wish,' he said.

She set the bath in front of the fire instead, not wanting him to risk a chill. Then she took her husband's accounts ledger and retired to the vestibule.

A short while later she heard him calling her. She went to him.

'A towel,' he said.

'Forgive me.'

She fetched one from the laundry cupboard and held it out for him. He wrapped it around his waist and climbed the stairs to his room.

That evening she also took a bath, adding dried lavender to the water. She was about to take his dinner up to his room when he appeared.

'Have you eaten yourself?' he asked.

She shook her head.

'Then join me.'

She set the table beside the fire and produced a bottle of wine from the supply which Thomas had always kept in their room.

'A toast,' she said, 'to a new season.'

He drank, and then they ate. Afterwards he sat down in the rocking chair and lit his pipe.

'How did your husband die?' he asked.

'A wasting disease, according to the village doctor.' She paused. 'More wine?'

He accepted a glass. She had been tempted to tell him about Marguerite but caution had prevailed. She drained her own glass and filled it up again.

Outside water was dripping from the eaves of the building. She had to bring the crow inside each evening, but the thaw was well advanced now and soon he would be able to spend the night beneath the moon. She drank more wine, studying her taciturn visitor and wondering whether he had a family. Something told her he came from the city, though whether he was travelling to or from there, she could not say.

The bottle was empty, and she fetched another from her room, telling him that it had always been their habit to share a bottle or two with their first guest of the season. He accepted another glass, but when that was empty would take no more.

She fell to talking of the villagers, telling him of their fears of the city and the strange stories they told of its inhabitants. She was hoping it would provoke some revealing comment from him, but he said nothing, puffing on his pipe and staring calmly at her as she spoke.

The wine had gone to her head, and her whole body felt warm. She undid a button at the neck of her shirt.

'Do you have a wife?' she asked.

'I spend much time travelling.'

He seemed content that this was answer enough; she did not prompt him.

'When did you marry?' he asked.

'Three years ago.'

'What brought you to this place?'

'My husband received an inheritance on our marriage and wanted to start a new life in a new place.'

Again he made no comment. She set her empty wine glass aside. 'Tell me, should I credit the stories which the villagers tell of the city?'

'It would be better to go there and form your own conclusions.'

'But are there such creatures as they speak of?'

'The only creatures I know are humans and animals.'

'But some have – special gifts?'

'Most surely. There are few anywhere who do not.'

The candle on the table guttered and went out, leaving them in the blood-orange light of the fire. Simon rose and tapped his pipe against the chimney, then bade her goodnight.

Stella sat staring into the fire, watching the flames devour the wood he had chopped for her. Eventually she rose and climbed the stairs. His room was in darkness, and when she knelt at the spy-hole, nothing could be seen.

That night she had a vivid dream of Marguerite and a guest who had stayed at the inn during the summer. Stella had forgotten his name, but he was a handsome young man whom Marguerite led to a large bed covered with tiny, writhing snakes. Then his face changed into that of another young man she remembered, and then another. As they lay down together, the dream slipped away

The next day she was able to uproot several turnips from the small garden which she cultivated at the rear of the inn. That afternoon she asked Simon if he would help her bury her husband.

She had not entered the cellar since the morning after the

snowstorm. Although the thaw was now well advanced, the cellar was still icy cold and her breath misted as she descended the stone stairway with Simon at her shoulder.

She had a sudden image of Thomas making love to her: he was a stout, red-faced man who snorted and panted, flecks of spittle gathering at the corners of his mouth, his eyes bulging. He lay on the stone slab where she had left him. The snow which had covered his body had hardened and crystallised during the winter so that he seemed to be encased in frosted glass. Then she saw that despite the coating of ice, a rat had gnawed away his face.

She tried to dislodge his body from the slab, but it would not budge. Silently she pleaded with Simon to help her, but he watched, unmoving, until finally she ran past him up the stairs.

He made her sit in an armchair and brought her a mug of strong, sweet tea. Then he returned to the cellar and brought the body up on the handcart which was used for moving wine casks. He took it outside and left it in the woodshed.

'We have to bury him,' she insisted.

He shook his head. 'Not until he's unfrozen.'

That evening the temperature dropped sharply and it began to snow.

Stella sat at the window, watching the world turn slowly white again. Simon had already retired, leaving his pipe on the arm of the chair. The fire in the hearth was dying; she added more wood before retiring to her room.

Through the spy-hole she saw him sitting in bed reading by candlelight. With the snowfall a pervasive silence seemed to have settled on the inn, and she had the impression that they were two people trapped, frozen in by the weather. She imagined Simon removing her husband's body from the wood-shed and chopping it into pieces which he then fed to the fire.

At length she undressed and got into bed. She always slept nude, piling more blankets on her bed as the winter advanced until she felt like an animal cocooned in a deep burrow. To her surprise, sleep came easily.

She dreamt of her husband, remembering the time in summer when a party of six guests had arrived, bound for the city. She had gone to fetch him to help prepare their rooms and had found him asleep on their bed, a winy vomit surrounding him. In her dream the vomit was the colour of bile, and when she rolled him over there was a dark hole where his face should have been. Then the young men of whom she had dreamt earlier were standing in the doorway, pointing at him and laughing. She was smiling at them.

Their laughter grew louder and more staccato until she became aware of a rapping on the door knocker downstairs. She went out into the empty corridor and descended the stairway without haste, her hand on the banister.

The moment she opened the door, the icy wind blew in a flurry of snow. Marguerite was standing there, dressed in white. Her face was as glacially beautiful and as timeless as ever. She smiled her irresistible smile, and Stella felt as if she was drowning in the blueness of her eyes. Then she entered, shaking the snow from her cloak.

Stella followed her like a sleepwalker as she passed through the vestibule, glancing at the empty hook on the key board. The faint aroma of Simon's pipe-smoking still lingered in the air. Silently Marguerite ascended the stairs.

She went directly to Simon's room and turned the handle. It opened without protest, closed behind her without a word. Stella stood outside, her mind blank. Then a shiver freed her from her numbness. She entered her own room and went directly to the spy-hole.

Everything was dark and silent in the room, but she had the strong impression of movement and life. She waited. Outside it had stopped snowing and a sickle moon shone bright between scudding clouds. The stars looked adamantine. She waited.

Abruptly Simon's room erupted with a brilliant white light which made her recoil from the spy-hole. There was a piercing scream which rent her mind like fingernails scraped on ice. And then silence.

The light continued to pour through the spy-hole as she cowered on the floor. Then, after a long time, it gradually began to fade to orange and then to red. The dimming of the light was slow, but Stella did not move. Nor did she entertain the thought of putting her eye to the spy-hole when it had died completely. Chilled to the marrow, she crawled into her bed.

Dawn seemed to come quickly, and she did not know whether she had slept or not. She lay there, watching the gathering of the light and the movement of clouds, patterns as fickle and inexorable as life itself. Beyond the wall there was no sound. The cradles of snow on the windowpanes began to melt under the sun.

At length she heard a movement next door. She waited. The door opened and footsteps receded in the corridor and down the stairs.

She crept to the spy-hole and peered through. The bed was unmade and the curtains had not been drawn. She could not be sure whether the tousled white sheets were darkened with shadows or a greyish dust.

She heard the crow give an enfeebled cry, and realised that she had forgotten to take him in that night. She hurried to the window.

Simon was walking through the melting snow towards the city road. She opened the window and found the air possessed of all the mildness which heralded a true spring thaw. His long cloak erased his footprints in the snow as he went.

Then she saw that he had taken Thomas from the woodshed and laid him on a pile of straw under the sun. His body already looked free of its surface coating of ice; a black cloth had been tied around his face. At the bottom of the garden Simon had dug a grave.

Before the sun set she would go down and give him a decent burial.

An apocryphal historic fantasy from Ian Watson, the award-winning author of *The Embedding*, *Miracle Visitors*, *Death-hunter* and many other popular novels. Ian lives with his wife and daughter in the Northamptonshire countryside where he writes full-time when not winning gardening prizes or standing for office in local politics.

In the Mirror of the Earth

Ian Watson

Raoul was a Sleeper: the first Sleeper I had ever come close to (in either the proximal or the emotional sense!) during all my years of wandering across Thraea.

Not, I hasten to add, that I journeyed in order to meet Sleepers, whom personally I had always regarded as pathological half-persons.

Besides, their whereabouts are well enough known to every child. No diligent search is necessary; though perhaps a fair deal of patience, ardent persuasion and even greasing of palms is a requisite *sine qua non* for actual admission into the presence of one of our pampered and protected treasures.

Who are to be found – all six of them currently, out of a world population nudging two billion souls – ensconced in their quaintly named Observatories in the capital cities of Atlantica, Pacifica, Indica, Mediterre and Baltica. (Oh yes, and there's one on the island of Caspia.)

Observatories, ah ha! I've sometimes wondered whether it is the Sleepers who are being observed there – or whether it is *they* who are doing the observing. Or both. Or both. Still, we Thraeans aren't an overwhelmingly superstitious people; so I suppose to describe those guarded palaces as 'Sleep Temples' or some such, and their attendants as 'priests' would hardly be deemed good form.

Though indeed, in so far as we do possess a secular religion – or maybe I should call it an 'imaginative mythology' – as anyone glancing at the place names on the map of the world must inevitably concur that we do, this is entirely owing to the observations of all the random generations of Sleepers; of whom sometimes as many as nine have at any one time been alive, and sometimes as few as one.

But never, as it happens, none. Would none be taken as a dire omen? By some, no doubt; by some.

Never none, as I say; and very rarely in our history only one. Imagine the feelings of that singleton! One solitary sport of nature, one peerless lonely caprice! What a fate.

But hush, I said that six Sleepers are alive today – in our present well-endowed epoch. Yet a seventh is also alive, far removed from any metropolitan Observatory, unknown but to my good self. Quite a life of danger and subterfuge is his: danger while he lies enslothed in what the mystic poets call 'slumber', and which more scientifically inclined spirits prefer to describe as 'rapport with the Submerged'; danger, also, from any of our dreams which happen to encounter him during his waking hours, against which he, unpractised and ill-equipped, obviously has no defence.

Peril, yes, and subterfuge – for our seventh secret Sleeper, Raoul.

Frankly, when I first found out his identity I was astonished that he did not surrender himself forthwith to the rich life: of servants, mistresses, excellent cuisine, dream-guards and all the rest of the panoply – for the simple *quid pro quo*, ego-flattering in itself, of having his words hung on till the end of his days by a retinue of scribes, sages, scoliasts and pilgrims.

Yet Raoul, it seemed, was in search of something of his own. As was I myself! Besides, his parents having by hook and by crook kept his sleeping sickness a dark secret, perhaps he also felt that he owed it to their memory to honour that unlucrative investment in his privacy.

Lucre . . . There, I've mentioned it; and I would rather that I hadn't. For this casts a tiny shadow of doubt on the altruism of my motives.

A handsome reward goes to the parents of a Sleeper as soon as they declare their child and hand him or her over into safe-keeping. Which has even led in the course of our history to one or two attempted masquerades. Naturally, such deceit is bound to fail; for even if the miscreant mother and father pretend to have been completely out of touch with all civilisation, stuck in some incredibly remote spot during the whole babyhood and infancy of their brat – till it reached an age when it could be trained to dissimulate – even so no child can possibly lie still with its eyes shut eight hours per day for a single week, let alone year in year out. Especially not for somebody else's benefit!

The question of lucre, though ... To my knowledge the situation had never arisen before, yet it seemed a fair presumption that a generous reward might equally well accrue to anybody delivering news of a rogue *adult* Sleeper at large.

However, Raoul had no need to fear my betraying him. And I'm sure that the thought never really crossed his mind, except perhaps at the very outset.

But first things first ...

I had been wandering for some years, as I say, paying my way where food wasn't free for the taking or impaling with my crossbow, by selling my dreams for show – and on occasion pitting them against other waking dreams in contest or combat; since my own dreams are particularly powerful, coherent projections.

Powerful, indeed ... But here I must emphasise that no Romantic am I. On the contrary! Dreams are a psychic superfluity; and my psyche happens to be particularly orderly. Thus my classic turn of mind produces strongly structured dreams which are, if I say it myself, a distinct cut above the slop that a lot of other people produce: outpourings of wobbling jelly, rather than creatures with real teeth, or objects with some design function to them.

Yes, I'm a classicist. Personally I've never felt inclined to warble song or revel in nature or cultivate ambiguous mysteries – unlike many other wanderers I have met with on my travels, not least of all those many perfervid pilgrims tramping their way from one Observatory to the next on the Grand Tour ...

I'm sure that the main advantage of having as many as six Sleepers in residence all over the world is that it keeps such folk on the move! If there were only one known Sleeper extant – in the city of Seashells, for the sake of argument – what a host of pilgrims would bunch up there like moths round a single lanthorn, like bees at the only available flower-bed!

No, it wasn't in poetry, nature or metaphysics that I found true beauty and significance, but rather in the engineering and civil architectural masterpieces of Thraea; and it was to admire and assess these that I travelled the globe, taking in, to name but a few highlights, the Panama Bridge that links Pacifica with Atlantica; and the Gibraltar Ship Canal down the frontier between Atlantica and Mediterre allowing boats of deepest draught to pass directly from the Gulf of Algeciras into the Bay of Tangier; and by no means least the might Suez Bridge joining Mediterre with the Peninsula of Suez, that long slim finger pointing from the crooked arm of Indica ...

Why didn't I settle down sooner to design something equivalent? Well, you know what they say: one leaves home in order to return; one ranges the whole wide world in search of oneself. So if I had sometimes asked myself that very question in weary or frustrating moments during my wander-years, the answer had to be that during all this time I was still matching myself against what had already been accomplished. I was still in pursuit of a project grand enough: one which no one had yet dared, or even be *able* to conceive.

Yet I realise that I have mentioned *Raoul*'s name – but not my own!

Enough. If you haven't already guessed it, my name is Tomas d'Arque – from which you will have no difficulty in pinning down my birthplace to a certain fair town in Liguria Province of Mediterre, not too far from Lake Corsica.

And this is how I first discovered Raoul's secret, and became for a while his elder brother, protector, confidant ...

It happened amid the seven hundred densely forested lakes of the Bahamas. Specifically it occurred some eight or nine miles north of the sporting resort of Providence, where the hunting is so well renowned, out in the woodland near North Bimini Pool.

I was on my way north to inspect the newly completed 150-mile-long dam built to drain the salty shallows of the Florida Polder, so that I could tick off one more engineering feat as not quite worthy of aspiring to. An admirable endeavour, to be sure! Make no mistake. Twenty long years it had taken. However, it was something which had already been dreamed, and done.

Here I must add an original insight of my own, stemming from my relationship with Raoul, concerning the surprise occasionally voiced by certain cultural historians that in our world where the tempo of life has ever remained demure, our people should nevertheless from quite early times constantly exhibit such devotion to mammoth, long-term feats of construction. I believe I know the real, *deep* reason why this is so.

Pray consider the way in which a Sleeper must view his life's span compared with all the rest of us. We are alive and conscious without ceasing; not even excluding the couple of hours every fortnight or so when we discharge our dreams (our psychic superfluity). Whereas he *dies* for eight hours out of every twenty-four, as regularly as clockwork.

For him the daily death of sleep – the robbery of time – may well breed a panic urgency, an inner allegiance to more short-term goals; to which I can juxtapose our own sense of continuity and connection, which breeds in us the desire to connect: capes of land with other capes by means of very long bridges or causeways; and the bay of one sea to the nearest bay of a neighbouring sea by means of grand canals – so that everything will flow and join together continuously.

Yet there's more. From what Raoul told me, a Sleeper's fleeting visions of the Submerged are somewhat confused and not quite under the control of his own will. Of course, it's otherwise with everyone else, particularly the more coherent spirits amongst us. So, being able to project in miniature a majestic bridge or other edifice, it is easy and logical to conceive of this project being carried through into actuality in brick and stone, somewhere appropriate upon the surface of Thraea; and a whole nation or city can easily be fired with a fine dreamer's vision, and act upon it. A powerful dream-projection readily becomes a building project.

Such was the case with the Swannee Project for damming and draining the Florida Polder, whither I was heading. Typically, the name seemed somewhat capricious, since neither the forests of Atlantica nor the grain-lands of Mexique to the west of the polder were noted for any such bird-life as swans! Yet this was the name which had been chosen metaphysically, by the Sleeper of Atlantica, during one of his nightly sorties into the Submerged...

Raoul, however. Raoul, and what happened near North Bimini Pool ...

I was riding my newly acquired bay gelding through dense woodland along a little-frequented bridle path. There was not *too* much danger of attack by angry boars or sore-headed bears; and by keeping to this byway I hoped to avoid any further encounters with brash sportsmen – who have even been known to try to pit their blundering dreams against savage prey, rather than use their crossbow bolts.

Ah, brash sportsmen: they have their uses, though! Only a few hours earlier in Providence I had obtained my fine mount and its full panniers as the result of a dream contest with one such . . .

Besides appealing to the hunting instinct, and to a modicum of gluttony upon the products of the chase, Providence also caters to gambling fever – which I suppose is a variant on the hunt, involving this time the bagging, or more often the escape of money. A famous casino, there, occupies the wives and girl-friends of the addicts of the chase; and after a few days in Providence the women seem willing to wager upon anything and everything. Will the hotel chef dish up that newly bagged boar with an orange or an apple in its mouth? Ten gives you twenty it'll be an apple.

I had felt my dream-time coming on as I tramped into Providence earlier on foot, and decided to capitalise on this, as I was somewhat strapped for funds. Luckily for me the casino was fresh out of a main act to amuse the guests, due to a bout of tummy upsets amongst a newly arrived team of artistes, who were no doubt unused to the rich fare. So the casino compère was only too happy to comply with my request.

As usual with such dreamshows – lest they get out of hand – the venue was the open air rather than upon the indoor stage; though in this case the open air was graciously accoutred with a marquee awning stretched above a natural grassy amphitheatre, and lit by many lanthorns.

Deliberately I had held back my dreams for a few hours longer than need be, to build their power and organisation; and as luck would have it none of the guests or staff were dreaming that evening – or else, if they were, they stayed discreetly indoors with their jejune projections.

All, that is, but for my sportsman; as I was to discover (to *his* cost) twenty minutes or so into my show.

First I projected before me a wondrous miniature city of considerable detail; and as soon as it was firm I invited selected members of the audience – the prettiest – down onto the floor of the amphitheatre to step along my city's boulevards and test the strength of its public buildings, before returning to their seats.

Allowing no fires to break out nor any tremors to escape into the audience, I then daringly destroyed my city in an earthquake.

For variety, next I dreamed a dancing, juggling bear. And it was at this point that the presumptuous oaf challenged me to a combat of dream-beasts, to the acclaim of his coterie of friends. I shan't expatiate upon his vivid but basically floppy projections. Suffice it to say that, having allowed him various vantages for the sake of his *amour-propre*, and to let wagers mount up, I trounced the fellow. The upshot for me: possession of that bay gelding, and full panniers.

So towards midnight I was about nine miles north of Providence, seated upon my spoils, occasionally checking that the bridle way ran true by reference to what stars I could spy through rifts in the foilage; when my keen sense of danger alerted me. That, and the snicker of the gelding.

Some way off the path in the dark underbrush I heard a grunt; then another. Reining in, as the rhythmic rasping noise continued, I reached for my crossbow, thinking: bear... or boar.

Another man might have ridden cautiously on; or, had his dreaming been upon him, as it was upon me earlier, he might have sent a dream-beast crashing through the dingy boscage; as it was, I was fresh out of dreams. And I must admit that my curiosity has led me into tight scrapes often enough in the past; this must go with being an inventive sort of fellow!

My steed pawed the turf, and whinnied; as I was hesitating a gibbous moon floated from behind some clouds, increasing the light. Recklessly I dismounted and tethered the gelding to a handy tree stump, soothing it, then I crept slowly into the underbrush, crossbow cocked, prepared to snatch back my foot should I feel a bending twig about to snap.

Ten steps, twenty; and a tiny clearing hove dimly in sight ... where, wrapped in a blanket, lay what I took at first sight to be a severely injured man in his death agony.

A few paces more, and the amazing truth dawned on me: that

the man was *sleeping* – the noise, as Raoul later explained, in some embarrassment, was that of 'snoring'. At his head, a knapsack.

What to do? I was consumed with curiosity, yet if I broke his sleep I could shock or injure him. After thinking this over, I sat down right there in the clearing and remained so all night long, till dawn began to creep into the east.

During my long hours of vigil – interrupted only by two forays: once to the horse for a bite of pasty and a swig of wine, and the second time into the bushes on a call of nature – I noted how the man did not lie entirely still in his comatose state. At times he shifted from one side to the other, as if by some automatic instinct of his muscles, to protect himself from cramp or gangrene. And twice he cried out: once, the word, 'Everglades', and on the second occasion as if in baby talk, 'Palm Beach, my Mammy!' 'Everglade' no doubt referred to the extensive woods we were in, in a submerged, mythistorical fashion; though as to the latter I knew of no palm-fringed shores closer than the equatorial strands of the South American Ocean, down Cayenne way.

As the forest cover eventually brightened I discerned that the Sleeper was only about twenty-one years old, with an unruly mop of dark hair, and fine, almost feminine features. When the bird chorus burst into song about us, he opened his soft brown eyes; and so we first met – much to his initial consternation.

Quickly I reassured him; though on awakening it seemed that the Sleeper was still quite confused as to the substantial reality of the world. So without further ado I set to and cooked us both a tasty breakfast of venison sausages. No doubt it was because I treated him thus in comradely style as just another person like myself, not as a wonder and a living miracle, that he soon began to warm to me and to consider me as a potential friend and ally after all his years of subterfuge and self-imposed isolation.

I did not just wag the ready ear of one who only listens in order to betray confidences and turn them to his own advantage; but I presented my own life's quest, and myself, to him, so that presently he began to trust me, and soon to see merits: such as a horse to ride in tandem with me, and best prospect of all, someone reliable to watch and ward him while he slept. That night, and the night after, and the night after that ...

By the time we arrived at Jack's Ville on the eastern shore of the Swannee Project a couple of weeks later, Raoul had already told me much about his relationship with the Submerged – which he had actually used, rather cunningly, as protective coloration. For he had long since adopted the guise of a rather devout mythistorical pilgrim.

Thus whenever he was obliged to rent a room in a town, he could perfectly excuse his otherwise peculiar custom of locking himself away for hours at a stretch: such were his times of obligatory meditation upon the enigmas of the Submerged and our mythistory.

Hard times, quite often! In a room intended to shelter ordinary travellers, what could Raoul lie down on but the floor? In the absence of female companionship he could hardly rent an amour-chambre; alone in a cushioned love-nest he would have been regarded as very weird indeed – and I suspect, though he didn't answer this question directly, that Raoul had even denied himself the joys of intercourse entirely, lest with his seed spilt and passion spent he might fall *asleep* in someone's arms. Till he met me it had been a sad life for him.

So we reined in on a low hilltop above Jack's Ville: that once tiny hamlet which had grown into something of a mini-city with all the construction work; and we both dismounted to survey the long dam stretching out forever to the west, straight as a die. To the south, the beginnings of the Polder; to the north the white breakers of the North American Ocean (for it was a breezy day).

Raoul stared fixedly southwards as though the dam itself meant nothing to him.

'Florida is rising,' he said. 'Rising into view. Wouldn't it be rare if there were drowned cities to be found beneath the sea?'

'And who would have built them?' asked I, laughing. 'Mermen?'

I began to speculate, though, whether it might not be a grand enough project to build something noble *underwater*: with fishes swimming beyond the toughened windows, and air pipes leading to the surface? No one had ever constructed anything beneath the waves. How would one go about it? By means of massive caissons? Or using a circular dam, which one later demolished to let the briny deep flow back in? As you can see, already my intimacy with Raoul was beginning to stir strange and wonderful imaginings within me – amply repaying the care I was lavishing on our relationship.

Raoul cleared his throat. 'Some pilgrims say that when the universe was made, another universe had to be made too, for balance. Or maybe this was because the universe is made out of the void, say others; for a void isn't just emptiness. You can tear it apart, into two distinct but complementary things: the Real and the Submerged, the Mythistorical. Yet there must be a place *somewhere*,' and he banged his fist into his palm, 'where the two join, if only as a thread, an umbilicus. A location. A door. Where land is sea, and sea is land, unseparated out.'

'Like a swamp, you mean? Ah, so that's why you were heading here now that we're pumping the Polder dry?'

From our vantage point we could clearly see the first of the great hydraulic stations two miles out along the dam; and less distinctly a second, and a third. I fancied that I could hear the thump and slosh of that first station like a distant heartbeat, powered by the spinning windmills on its roof. Bucket by bucket, at fifty such locations, Florida was being emptied out, reclaimed for Atlantica; and during a few moments of reverie I was overwhelmed by the certainty that here, for the first time in history, the actual geography of Thraea was being slightly modified; so that what had been coloured blue on maps hitherto, now would be painted green. Fortunately my sense of proportion soon reasserted itself.

Raoul gripped my arm. 'I wonder if that dam can really hold? There must be so much pressure of water against it!'

I assessed the structure with a practised eye.

'It looks well enough built. Yet perhaps it shouldn't be so utterly *straight*. That might encourage waves to build up abnormally high as they roll along it in the winter. Whereas if they'd built it with curving bays, giving it a scalloped edge, or if they'd thrust groins out, which could have served as piers sometime in the future. . .'

His grip tightened. 'I wonder what other pressures are thrusting against it? Pressures, perhaps, from the Submerged itself. . . Imagine the inundation if the dam does break!'

'Oh, then you'd have land and sea mixed up all right, in one almighty pudding! But let's not carp at the workmanship, just because the design seems so linear and monotonous. It reflects, after all,' and I winked wickedly, 'our sense of continuity; whereas the periodic pump-stations, throbbing away − not unlike somebody *snoring* . . . ' I nudged him in the ribs affectionately, just as he released my arm. 'Enough said!'

We remounted one behind the other, and rode on down together into Jack's Ville.

That same night Raoul cried out the one strange word in his sleep, several times: 'Okefenokee!' In the morning over a breakfast of muffins, bacon and cinnamon coffee, I questioned him.

He shrugged fretfully. 'Another of the place names of the Submerged, Tomas! Somewhere hereabouts . . . '

'But,' I asked him trenchantly, 'will it *still* be submerged, now that hereabouts is being drained? In a word, is "Okefenokee" the name of the door to your destiny?' (Several words, actually. But I thought I phrased it rather well.)

He stared blankly, hardly focusing. 'How would it be,' he muttered at last, 'to tread the Submerged lands? Would the denizens of the Submerged perceive us as ghostly wraiths? Spooks, or will o' the wisps? Vague blobs of light, occasionally solidifying into seemingly solid people? And what would they make of your projected dreams? Would these seem to be silver elves and hunking, dripping giants, and mothmen and such?'

'Do you *really* believe in the existence of these . . . counter-people?'

'Counterfeit people?' He misunderstood me, or deliberately chose to do so. 'I must be one of those myself, born into the wrong universe!'

'Surely,' said I reasonably, 'the Submerged is simply our mythic dimension? It's like a sort of fifth dimension of our world, Raoul. The bulk of people only notice four dimensions: length and breadth and time and height. But there's another one, as well, which *you* perceive − perhaps it's required as a kind of glue to join the other four together. Let its name be *depth*; depth is different in nature from height.'

'Height?' he retorted, as though I had offended him. 'Fat lot you know about height! Length and breadth and time, oh yes. But height? I'll give you height!'

'Now what would you mean by that?' I asked soothingly.

And he told me; and it came as a revelation.

Not, I hasten to add, because *he* intended it as such; but because then and there at once I was able to grasp that this was the missing piece in the puzzle of my life. With an instinctive sense of right structure I slotted that piece straight into place; and thrilled.

I did not tell Raoul that I had experienced revelation, due in small part to him. I feared that this might make him vain and swollen-headed with a sense of his own importance; which could in turn have made him reckless. So, while my brain buzzed inwardly with a grand conception, I simply nodded.

'There's something in that,' I allowed; and I ruffled his hair. 'Care for another muffin?'

That all took place four years ago.

I still can't believe that Raoul deliberately gave me the slip that day in Jack's Ville due to some paranoid suspicion that I might betray his identity. Still less could it have been caused by any disinclination for my company, since I was proving to him for the first time in his lonely life how valuable friendly human brotherhood can be. For a while I suspected that something ill had befallen him.

But now I realise why he went, and where he is to this very day.

Even now it will take several more years to drain the Florida Polder entirely since the water level only sinks slowly, even with fifty bucket-stations on the job. So the Polder is still betwixt and between: a queer region of salt swamp, neither properly land nor water, full of dead rotting seaweeds and the bones of fishes beached on newly arisen cays.

I *know* that, haunted by inner necessity, Raoul will be the wanderer of that half-land. He will be blowing into empty conch shells to harken for an answering echo from somewhere in the murk, and to follow it, there to fall asleep and listen to the whisper of metaphysical names – some of which the Sleeper of Atlantica is already enunciating publicly: Canaveral, Tampa, Orlando, Lauderdale ...

I take note of these announcements, even back home here in Mediterre; though I must confess that I'm not *consumed* with curiosity. These days I have my own work cut out – ever since my own grand dream-projection, and accompanying passionate explanations, convinced the good folk of my native Liguria to undertake the work.

For what I realised during my moment of revelation in Jack's Ville was that all the great engineering projects of Thraea hitherto have been concerned exclusively, and mundanely, with length and breadth and time – with connecting land mass to land mass, and linking ocean to ocean. Never have we dreamed of connecting the ground *to the sky* in a purely gratuitous aesthetic way with no strict linear purpose.

Already here in Liguria midway between Lake Corsica and the Azure Coast the foundations and base of my tower are complete, and the first stage will soon be rising.

To begin with, I thought of naming it the 'Eiffel Tower', after a phrase that spilled from Raoul's lips once while he was asleep – followed the next morning, on enquiry, by a description of a most unusual erection.

Yet on second thoughts I have decided not to use any Submerged name; for on the contrary *my* creation will soar upward and upward. So instead, I may well call it 'Raoul's Tower' to honour a well-loved if briefly known friend; thus to tantalise all future visitors, without betraying any confidences.

Though somewhere in the structure – well concealed in a strong casket, yet so placed that a future generation will come upon it while refurbishing some part of the fabric, thus unlocking an enigma of years – I shall secrete this true account of the genesis of my masterpiece. Which will inevitably be a Wonder of the World.

On the other hand, though, if I *do* call it 'Raoul's Tower', future biographers may leap to the conclusion that Raoul was my lover during our brief sojourn together; or even that I may have taken advantage of him while he *slept*! That lays *too* much stress upon our relationship.

So on balance maybe the 'Tomas Tower' is the better name; and if I deliberately leave my work untitled – thus emphasising its nonfunctional purity – so it will inevitably come to be known. People are impelled to give names to things; what other *raison d'être*, I sometimes wonder, is there for our precious Sleepers in their Observatories?

Tomas Tower: I think I like it. But let time and history decide.

And to time and the future I bequeath this little memoir: to a posterity when maybe – though I doubt it – the world will have changed out of recognition; for which reason, pardon me my explanations of items that will surely appear to you completely obvious and well known.

Such as my own name:

(signed with a flourish)

Tomas d'A.

'John Grant' is the pseudonym used by an ex-publisher now writing full-time down in Devon. He is the co-editor (with Colin Wilson) of *The Book of Time* and *The Directory of Possibilities* and author of *A Directory of Discarded Ideas* and *The Book of Numbers*. This rare fiction outing examines the perennial theme of the unicorn from a somewhat humorous angle.

When All Else Fails

John Grant

'Danger,' said Seth's voice in my mind, so I pulled him over to the side of the glade and waited, listening. Just ahead of me Alla, hearing us come clinking to a halt, reined in her horse, Fireflight; he snorted a couple of times, but she soothed him quietly, and he fell silent. We waited motionlessly, listening to the sounds of the birds and the rustle of summer leaves.

'What is the danger?' I thought to Seth. 'I can't hear anything.'

'They're close,' he replied. 'About ten or a dozen of them. A hunting party, I think. They seem very stupid.'

Alla looked at me. I shrugged, pointed at Seth's head, then put a finger to my lips.

'They're not hostile, exactly,' came Seth's cool voice, 'just greedy. They've seen me and they want me. You could climb down from me and ride off with Alla on Fireflight – they wouldn't stop you.'

'And leave a friend?'

'They're well armed. And there are more of them than you.'

'But stupid.'

'There is that.' Seth made that funny feeling in my mind that told me he was laughing.

I smiled. 'I should think Alla is worth about twenty of them, whoever they are. *Where*ver they are is more important: ahead of us or behind?'

'That's the problem,' thought Seth. 'I can't quite work it out. It's always easier to pinpoint intelligent minds: stupid ones just create a sort of mist. But they're very close – close enough to see us clearly.' His great white head scanned from side to side across the glade. 'I'm trying to work out the angles they're looking at us from – it's so hard when I can only pick up glimpses through their eyes.'

I winced at an unexpected sound, my hand shooting to

Windrush's hilt, then realised that it was only Alla drawing Killer from his scabbard; in the bright sunlight his blade flickered on the border of visibility and invisibility.

'I have one,' thought Seth, a rare note of excitement creeping into his touch. 'Over there, behind that clump of gorse.'

Windrush's dull, black evil blade now waved in the air; he was eager to taste a soul. 'On the count of three,' I said to Alla, my voice only just above a whisper. 'One, two . . .'

My head exploded.

I was awoken by the stink: a mixture of rotting food, unwashed humanity, festering turds and an underlying stratum of general squalor. My head was a jumbled tangle of confused thoughts – mainly my own. I searched around for Seth but could feel him nowhere; then opened my eyes reluctantly to dank light.

I lay on the floor of a hut that was as attractive as a privy. Clearly the branches had not been allowed to dry out properly before the walls had been built, for everywhere one looked there was the pale glow of fungus. There were two windows, just large enough to show that the sunlight was bright outside, just small enough to ensure that very little of that brightness was allowed in. The centre of the hut was a little higher than a tall man's head, and from it descended the walls in irregular arches to the ground; from side to side, the hut at its broadest was perhaps about two man-heights. The floor testified rather too plainly to the fact that the hut had been used for animals in the recent past. The straw was old, and damp with rot.

My hands had been tied behind my back, but my legs had been left unfettered and so it was not too difficult to wriggle myself up into a sitting position. In the gloom I could see that Alla must have returned to consciousness a little before me, because she was already making some progress towards loosening her bonds.

'Do you realise you snore when you've been knocked unconscious?' she said brightly.

I shook my head foolishly.

'It gave the Hax hunters a shock, I can tell you. They stood around prodding you for a while to make sure you weren't some kind of monster disguised as a man.'

'What happened?' I said.

She giggled: there must have been some blood. 'They caught us both simultaneously with thrown hammers,' she said. 'You were hit plum on the back of the head, and went down as if you were trying to make a hole in the ground. You did look funny.'

'I'm glad I entertained you.'

'I was luckier. The thing caught me only a glancing blow, but that was enough to knock me off Fireflight's saddle; by the time I'd recovered my senses the Hax had me tied up and were looking at this grunting monster . . .'

'But how did they get so near to us?' I turned my back on her and began to inch towards her. 'If they were close enough to throw hammers at us Seth should have been able to isolate them from the trees.'

'That was the problem . . . Thanks.' My fingers were beginning to pick at her bonds. 'The Hax and the trees have a very good understanding. The trees were creating a smokescreen, so that most of the minds that Seth was feeling weren't really there at all. Trees can be bastards like that, sometimes.'

One by one, the knots were yielding. It was hard work, picking away at them with fingers constrained by my own lashings, and sweat was already running down my forehead and into my eyes. I shook my head sharply to try to shake the worst of it away. 'So we didn't put up much resistance between us, my love?'

'Not very much – although the swords had a better time of it than we did . . . before they ran out of our mindstuff. I think Windrush got one, and Killer got two or three – one of them a beauty.' She giggled again and my stomach tensed. 'Stuck him in the groin and ripped straight up to his jaw,' she said. 'Guts everywhere.'

In a future age I would have realised with sudden shock that the lady I loved was a psychopath, but in the here and now I was only too anxious merely to change the subject. 'Where are the swords now?'

'Tied up in some other part of the village. I'm not sure exactly where: they're both very tired and it's hard to make out exactly what they're thinking. Seth and Fireflight escaped, though.'

'Thank God for that,' I said. 'I think if you wriggle your right

– no, hang on: it would be your left – your left hand just a little *that* way it should come free.'

With a jerk she pulled the hand clear of the tangle of cords and immediately began to worry her other hand free. 'Just be a moment,' she said. 'It's Seth who's the problem, really.'

'Yes, he told me. They want his horn.'

'You can hardly blame them, really. Tatty little village like this – that horn could keep them in luxury for a couple of years. Except that one of the local lords would be bound to hear about it and put them all to the sword to get hold of it.' I felt her fingers at mine. 'I tried to explain that to the Hax as they went charging off into the greenery after him, but their only response was to knock me unconscious again. More effectively, the second time.'

'You're certain he stayed free?' Already the bundle of cords at my back was beginning to feel softer.

'Quite certain,' she said, absentmindedly kissing the back of my neck. 'I heard a couple of them cursing about it just outside the window a few minutes before you woke up. Anyway, can you feel him?'

'No.'

'Then why did you ask?'

'He might already have been dead.'

'Oh. Sorry.' She struggled silently with the knots. I was beginning to feel desperately the need to urinate. A few moments later she spoke again: 'He and Fireflight are bound to try to get us out of here, you know.'

'Yes, and they'll be unsuccessful, and they'll get caught, too.'

'Precisely. Oh, sod this bloody thing. I reckon we'd be best to try to escape from the village before they make their attempt. There goes another fingernail.'

'How well are the Hax armed? I wish we knew exactly where the swords were.' I did, too: like any man uncertain of his virility, I always feel twice as aggressive when I hold Windrush in my hands.

'Primitive stuff, mostly,' she said. 'Throwing-hammers and axes. If they have bows I didn't see any. Spears, but not very straight ones, so I shouldn't think they'll be much of a problem. The real difficulty is that, at a guess, there must be a couple of hundred able-bodied men and women in the village – quite enough to deal with us even if their most deadly weapons were bananas.'

'Horses?'

'Not that I saw. I told you – it's a very crummy, poor little village. If Seth and Fireflight were here we could simply outrun them. There: you're free.'

'If Seth and Fireflight were here there wouldn't be any problem in the first place,' I said, rubbing my wrists, 'if you see what I mean. Is this hut safe? I mean, can we speak freely in it?'

'Yes,' she said, drawing me to my feet and giving me an affectionate hug. 'That was one of the first things I checked on waking up. It's neutral: doesn't like the Hax much, doesn't like us much, doesn't like anybody very much – I get the impression it thinks of human beings as a lower order of life.'

Alla is a very much better mind-toucher than I am. Of course, I am very close to Seth, so that often our minds become sufficiently mingled as almost to become one; and, like any fighter, I can touch Windrush, my sword. Otherwise, though, I must rely upon the evidence of my more mundane senses. Alla, on the other hand, can touch the minds of almost all things except, of course, other human beings ... and, curiously enough, Seth. I think it's possible that, in general, unicorns cannot be touched: a long time ago Seth must have decided that he liked me and would like to adopt me as a pet, and allowed me to touch him just for the fun of it. Now our relationship had changed: no longer was he the master and I the favoured animal; we were friends.

'Alla,' I said, 'I think our best chance of getting away from here is by using diplomacy.'

'"Diplomacy!"' she snorted, throwing her head back and looking at me as if I were insane. 'These primitives don't know the meaning of the word!'

'That's exactly why they're likely to be vulnerable to a little perverted use of it,' I said. 'They don't seem to be a particularly unpleasant lot – if they were they'd have killed us rather than just knock us about – '

'Unless, of course, they're planning some really exciting way of killing us,' said Alla. She could understand that. I wondered, just for a moment, if one day she would allow herself to be tortured to death if only for the pleasure of watching it happen.

'There's a chance of that, I suppose; but let's not think about it for the moment. Let's stick with the idea that they hold nothing against us, that all they want is Seth's horn. They can't know that Seth and I can touch – and they probably have never heard of mindstuff-swords, either. I think the easiest way of getting out of here is simply to ask them if they'll let us go.'

'Some hope! Besides, I want to kill a few – quite a lot, if possible.' She bit her lower lip and pouted slightly, looking all of sixteen.

'No, think of it from their point of view. If they let us go, either we'll just drift off or we'll lead them to Seth.'

'But we *would* lead them to Seth!'

'So we might. But once we're with Seth and Fireflight again, we can show them a clean pair of heels.'

She nodded, considering. 'I suppose so ... Doesn't sound much fun, though. Could we come back later and put the village to plunder?'

'My God, Alla, you're so blasted bloodthirsty!' I said. 'As you said yourself, anyone in the Hax's position would want to lay hands on a unicorn – it could mean that none of them would ever go hungry again. They're not basically evil people ... or, at least, I hope they're not.' And, in fact, I did have some sympathy for the Hax. Once this land was rich in unicorns, but then people found out that the ground horn could be used to make an aphrodisiac of inconceivable power. Soon the gentle creatures were being hunted down by everyone from Queen to pauper. When the supplies of the powdered aphrodisiac began slowly to become exhausted, people looked up dazedly from their frenzied rutting to find that there were no longer any unicorns to be found. Or, at least, that there were only a few. Those few had, understandably, learned to become elusive creatures, living only in the desolate lands and fleeing from the merest rumour of the coming of mankind.

Seth, impatient of the fugitive's life, had decided on the alternative approach. He had got hold of a vicious guard dog: me.

'You always say ... ' she said, then stopped, eyes going

slightly blank. 'They're taking Killer and Windrush some-where,' she said. 'The swords aren't sure where – the Hax have thrown them in the back of a wagon under some cloths. They think there are four Hax with them: two to pull the wagon and two to clear the forest ahead. Have you finished peeing yet? If we're going to be here any length of time we might as well agree both to use the same corner.'

As she squatted, arranging her feet fastidiously, I wandered over to one of the windows and looked out of it aimlessly. The scene that met my eyes was much as I'd expected: these hill villages are all much the same. But this was a larger one than usual. Assuming that I could see about half of the village, it must contain nearly a hundred living huts, as well as the usual few larger ones. Smoke rose from cooking fires: I reckoned it must be coming towards the evening of the summer's day. There were fewer young people around than one might have imagined at this time of day: presumably the party searching for Seth was a large one. Despite the size of the village, though, there were about it all the marks of poverty: no horses, and very few cattle or goats that I could see. I sniffed the air – few if any pigs, either. Seth's horn – or, at least, the wealth that it would bring – would mean a lot to those people.

Unfortunately, it meant a lot to Seth, too. Unicorns cannot survive without their horns. No one is quite sure why. At first sight it might seem that the horn is no more essential to the unicorn than a cow's horns to the cow; but, however carefully one tries to remove it, the creature lives for only moments without it. Worse still, from Seth's point of view, was the fact that according to the unicorn lore which he believed unques-tioningly the horn of a unicorn contains its soul: a unicorn that has lost its horn will wander forever halfway between the worlds of the living and of the dead, eternally unfulfilled. When I told Seth, once, that his ancestors had been hunted almost to extinc-tion because their horns contained a powerful aphrodisiac, he replied that that was only to be expected: the horns were filled with soulstuff, and soulstuff is the stuff also of life.

I turned from the window. Alla was kneeling in the centre of the floor, in silent conversation with a rat which had entered the hut. She gestured me to be silent – although of course I knew better than to interrupt her at a time like this. After a few moments she turned towards me.

'This friend tells me that Killer and Windrush are being taken to a clearing a little way from the village, and that we are to be set free to join them. He doesn't know why this should be, and I find it a little hard to fathom, myself.'

'Unless they've caught ...?'

'He tells me he's almost certain they haven't.' She caressed the little creature's head, and he turned and was gone in a blur through a crack in the corner.

The door opened.

At first I could see very little: although only a few moments before I had been looking out of the window at the brightly lit village scene, my eyes had already adjusted once more to the hut's gloom. My hands reached instinctively to my side for Windrush, but of course he wasn't there.

Alla presented herself much more coolly to our visitors. In contrast to my twitching and blinking, she simply drew herself to her full height and stared them in the eyes. Now that my vision had returned to normal I could make out that there were three of them – although behind them, outside the door, there was a throng of a couple of dozen ugly looking warriors, brandishing spears. I was not in the least happy.

'I hope for your sakes that you plan to set us free,' said Alla, not a tremor in her voice. 'I suppose you've realised that you've captured a noblewoman and her consort.'

'We beg your apologies, m'lady,' said the foremost of the three suavely. He looked not in the least perturbed by her hauteur: anywhere else but in a scrubby little village in the back of beyond he might have become a leader of men. 'My name's Parra, and I'm what passes as the chieftain of this mob.' He gestured with his hand to include the village. 'My patrols were out looking for robbers and, when they came across you, they decided to act first and think about it afterwards. If you really want me to, I'll have them flogged for the misdemeanour, but personally I'd rather not. We have too many robbers in these parts, and I'd just as soon not punish enthusiasm. Besides, we don't much go in for corporal punishment in this village, and

I'm not sure if I could easily lay hands on something suitable to have them flogged with.'

'There is no need to punish your men,' I interpolated, just before Alla could begin to insist that the hunters responsible be flayed alive – and by her, personally. Our way out of this mess was to let the fiction of Parra's explanation – and he was perfectly aware of the fact that we knew it was a fiction – be accepted as the basis for negotiation. 'We quite understand the position. If you'll just let us go free with our swords and our mounts and our belongings – why, I'm sure that the lady Alla and myself will soon have forgotten the whole incident.'

A pained look crossed Parra's face. 'Your swords, yes ... we have taken some precautions as regards your swords, but don't worry, you'll get them back. As for your mounts: well, the situation's not quite that simple.'

'Oh, yes?' said Alla, with dangerous drowsiness. I wished that human beings could touch each other, so that I could have told her to shut up.

Parra gave her a dirty look, then said to me: 'I'm afraid your mounts, in all the confusion, fled off into the forest. I've had a search party out these last few hours, looking for them so that we could give them back to you, but they've found nothing.'

'And I suppose, you slimy, two-faced bastard,' said Alla, losing the painfully thin veneer of tact to which she had been so amateurishly clinging, 'none of your blockheaded odoriferous bully-boys mentioned to you that one of those mounts is a unicorn?'

'Why, yes,' said Parra pleasantly, as if this were all just a light conversation at the market-place, 'I do believe that one of them did mention something like that. But, m'lady, what of it?'

'Alla, be quiet,' I said sharply. Our partnership was a successful one because she was skilled in battle while I was skilled in the more subtle war of words. 'I think that this noblewoman is suggesting that perhaps your motives are a little deeper than you claim.'

'Perhaps you're right.'

'You might almost say that she is implying that, since you've completely lost the unicorn, your only hope of ever seeing it again is to set us free, then follow us.'

'Well, we would hardly be human if it hadn't crossed our minds that out of this unfortunate accident our village might gain a little profit.' He smiled graciously. I liked him: he was rather like myself − one part coward, one part crook, and one part friend to anyone. I hoped that Alla or I wouldn't have to kill him.

'In those circumstances,' I said, 'the only possible course of action open to you *is* to set us free. You gamble that when we find our mounts your people can overcome us; we gamble that they can't. I don't think that there's any need for us to be unpleasant about all this.'

'Spoken like a man after my own heart,' he said with a broad, insincere leer − and it was then that I noticed the middle-aged woman standing beside and slightly to the rear of him. She might once have been beautiful but, if so, it had been a long time ago. Her eyes were like toad's eyes: shrewd, unblinking, taking in everything. I suddenly realised that Parra was merely her lips.

'Well, what's keeping us?' I said. 'If I were you I'd have taken our swords a few miles out into the forest, on the basis that if you gave them to us here we might get carried away and slit the old gizzard or two. So why not get right on and tell us where the swords are so that we can reach them by nightfall?'

'Why, certainly my friend,' he said. 'My people will follow you stealthily, of course, in the hope that you have some way of calling your mounts. If so, then our gamble can begin. That is fair?'

'Yes. Of course it is,' I said, but my intuition was screaming at me: *No, it isn't*. My intuition was rewarded with the slightest crinkling of the woman's eyes: Parra might think that that was all there was to it, but she knew better. There was something more.

A while later, Parra and his little party, together with the spear-brandishing warriors − rent-a-threat, as I might have thought a couple of millennia later − left us at the edge of the forest. Still I couldn't understand the woman's smugness: if she were as clever as she seemed, surely she must realise that two mounted people armed with mindstuff swords could easily slaughter the Hax several times over, if they wanted to − which Alla most obviously did. But she didn't seem to care.

I dropped my shoulders in pretended dejection and looked at her. 'Mother,' I said, 'there is something which you haven't yet told us, isn't there?'

For an instant the wrinkles around her eyes deepened: she was laughing at us.

'Why, yes, there is,' she agreed in a voice like the wind stirring up autumn leaves. 'You see, in the next village but one there is a virgin of marriageable age. And we are bringing her here.'

Neither Alla nor I could say anything: we just watched the group turn and make their way back towards the village of the Hax. What a lousy stroke of luck!

In no age have virgins of marriageable age been common, even the most superficially straitlaced. Boy-virgins, yes, for males have shynesses that females never dream of; but girl-virgins – no, they are a rare breed. I tell a lie: for a few decades there were plenty of girl-virgins of marriageable age around, those decades between the discovery of the aphrodisiac properties of unicorn's horn and the realisation that unicorns were virtually extinct. Then a girl-virgin could make herself a fortune in a few short years. Unicorns are, you see, addicted mind-touchers – and the one type of mind which they cannot resist touching is that of a woman who has reached marriageable age and yet has remained virgin. I suppose it's something to do with the incongruity of the whole situation: any woman can find a man who is only too willing to sleep with her, and human beings would not be human beings if they weren't curious enough to try out the unknown, sex, *once*. Even Seth, after his long association with one particular human mind, my own, would be unable to resist the lure of this novel experience: the touching of the mind of a girl-virgin of marriageable age. Confront a cat with a roomful of tame mice and it will forget for a little while that it really is a great friend of the cat next door.

'I think we've been outwitted,' I said to Alla.

'Possibly,' she said, but she didn't sound as hopeless as I'd expected. 'Say, I thought I did pretty well back there – acting the bloodthirsty woman.'

'You *are* a bloodthirsty woman.'

'Yes, I know. But I thought it was lovely the way they were all nervous in case I cut loose with my bare hands. And you, oh you were the sensible fellow who could keep me in check. Oh, how they wanted to keep you happy!'

'Actually,' I said, 'it was a pretty good performance. You came across as having the brains of a killer shark.' In spite of the fact that we had to do some rapid thinking, I speculated about the possibility of making love.

'I don't think we have time,' she said, reading the lines of my face. 'The first thing we have to do is circle the village and see what happens.'

'Shouldn't we find Fireflight and Seth?'

'Fireflight tells me that Seth has already found out about the virgin. He and Seth are over there – ' she gestured towards the far side of the village ' – waiting for the virgin to appear. Fireflight's tried to get Seth away, but it's no use.'

'Oh, rats!' I said, kicking a lump of earth.

Seth's mind touched mine before I could see him. 'Hello, there, brother,' he thought. 'I know you'll think I'm a fool, but . . . '

'I'm doing my best to understand,' I thought. 'Nevertheless, wouldn't everything be much simpler if we just put a few hundred leagues between us and this village?'

'Easier said than done, if you'll pardon the cliché,' thought Seth. 'The trouble with us unicorns is that we're predictable. Just as much so as are you humans. Put you out in the desert for a few days and then tell you there's a glass of water nearby . . . well, it's just the same with unicorns and virgins. I *can't* leave now that I know she's going to be here.'

Alla and I were fighting our way through a particularly dense patch of foliage at the time, so it was difficult to make myself heard above our collected grunts of effort, but I told her what Seth was thinking. 'Ask him if he can hold out for a day or two,' she said.

I touched Seth with the question. 'Why, yes, I suppose so,' he said, and he made that peculiar feeling which told me he was laughing. 'But what good would it do? I might as well be dead right now.'

'Would you like us to kill you, as soon as we see you, Windrush and I?' I asked. 'At least then you'd still have your horn.'

'You are kind, my friend, but no. I've never come across a virgin of marriageable age before; just touching her will give my life meaning. I would rather lose my soul than die before I'd ever found fulfilment.'

A few moments later Alla and I broke through the undergrowth to find Fireflight and Seth in front of us. The next couple of minutes were lost in all the trivialities of reunion: in particular, the swords, whose understanding is rather limited at the best of times, were overjoyed to see the animals, whom they had assumed to be lost to them forever. After a while, though, Alla and I found ourselves with our backs propped against a tree, chatting.

'Looks like Seth's had it,' I said gloomily.

'Oh, I wouldn't say that,' she said. 'You do realise that it's in your power to save him.'

'What?'

'Why do you think I wanted to know if Seth could force himself to stay away from the virgin for a couple of days?'

'I don't know. I thought it was a pretty pointless question, myself.'

'Well, it wasn't. I do wish you could get over your stereotyped image of me. Just because I'm beautiful and bloodthirsty doesn't mean I don't have a brain. There's a very easy solution: get rid of the virgin.'

'You mean: kill her?'

'That would be one way of doing it – but I don't think Seth would ever forgive you. Even though he's never touched her, he's hopelessly in love with her. That's the way with unicorns. I was thinking more in terms of getting rid of her virginity.'

I looked at Alla with a certain doubt. To say that she is jealous would be doing her a disservice through the sheer force of understatement ... although, as is the usual way with such things, she sees nothing anomalous in her being allowed to swipe whoever she wishes – and tell me all the details afterwards. But ... but I remembered the dancing girl in Haraf Mar, and I shuddered. 'Are you proposing that I should seduce her?' I asked.

'That would seem to be the easiest plan,' she said, leaning her head back and half closing her eyes, as if becoming bored with the whole subject. 'I'm surprised you didn't suggest it yourself.'

I was only too well aware of what would have happened had I

suggested it myself, but I let that pass. 'It's not going to be easy,' I said. 'I'll have to infiltrate the Hax, get close to her, and then work my wondrous charm. They're bound to keep a guard on her.'

'Yes,' she said, 'and you will be that guard. Sort out the details for yourself: I'm sleepy.' Like a cat she turned over on her side, curled up into a lazily elegant ball, and fell asleep. I didn't.

I paced nevously up and down outside the virgin's hut, shivering a little in the cold night air. So far, everything had gone according to plan. Becoming a member of the Hax had not been difficult – it's surprising how much difference a good layer of dirt can make to a man's appearance – and being selected as a guard had been almost automatic, since I am well built and muscular while the average member of the Hax is not. I knew that if I ever let myself get too close to Parra or the sinister woman I would be discovered, but so far it hadn't been too hard to blend into the background whenever they were nearby.

All of this sounds improbably simple, and it was. As mentioned earlier, the Hax were incredibly stupid people.

I thought of Alla, probably nestling in sleep against Fireflight's flanks, occasionally, without waking, soothing Killer and Windrush, both of whom suffered terribly from nightmares. I thought of Seth, his feet hobbled and his neck tied tightly to a tree. But I didn't think of them much, because most of my mind was occupied with thoughts of the virgin who slept just a few feet away from me, through the thin walls of the mud-and-branches hut.

Her name was Gurt, and she was not a virgin by choice.

They say that any woman can seduce any man, given enough time: I myself had been a practising homosexual before Alla had come along and taken me under her wing (and elsewhere). But Gurt was without a doubt the exception. It wasn't so much her individual features – some women veritably flaunt their beards or their toothlessness, and are all the more sexually desirable because of it – it was the overall cast of her mind. I can equably entertain the prospect of going to bed with anybody, no matter what they look like, either male or nowadays female (except Alla won't let me), so long as I am assured of the fact that they are fairly likeable, friendly people: while it may not reach the heights of a grand night of passion, a chummy romp is a great deal of fun. But this I could not envisage with Gurt. She kicked children when no one was looking, pulled the limbs off flies and other small animals, spat into other people's food for the sheer evil pleasure of it ... Earlier in the day I had seen her abuse her temporary power by ordering some poor Hax child to cover his face with faeces; quaking in case he offended the virgin, he had had to obey, to her shrill cackles of mirth. I couldn't imagine why Seth had the slightest desire to mind-touch her: certainly the prospect of merely body-touching her was giving my stomach some tremors.

However, with his consent, Alla had taken the tiniest of scrapings from Seth's horn – I think she had foreseen that there might be problems of this sort. For the thousandth time I felt in the pocket of my loincloth to make sure that the folded paper packet was still there: two specks of unicorn's horn, one for me and one for Gurt (in the remote event that she might prove intractable), each of them worth a small fortune.

I had just raised my fist to knock at the door of the virgin's hut when a thought struck me. There was absolutely no reason why *I* should be the man with whom Gurt lost her virginity ... and just then, by one of those happy coincidences which are always happening to me, I heard drunken footsteps approaching. I turned and in the wan light of the Moon I could see that it was Parra himself, no doubt having left some celebratory carousal briefly in order to do his duty, to see that all was well with the virgin's hut. He staggered towards me.

'Hello there, guard,' he said. 'Is everything well?' His eyes screwed up as he tried to make out my features, but the paucity of the lighting and the amount of alcohol he had consumed no doubt combined to render my face an anonymous blur, for he showed no signs of recognition.

I pulled myself to attention. 'Not a stir from within or without, sir,' I said preciesely, 'but it's bloody cold out here.'

As I had hoped, he pulled a leather flask from his pocket and offered it to me. 'Here's something to take the edge off the cold, soldier,' he said.

I took a sip, making it sound like an enthusiastic gulp, and then, while we chatted aimlessly about this and that, I slipped one of the scrapings of Seth's horn into the flask. I passed it back to him uncorked; with the automatic reaction of the totally intoxicated, he took a swig. I chose that instant to open the door of the virgin's hut.

The effect was amazing. Parra shot onto his tiptoes, let out a piercing shriek, and fell flat on the ground where he lay quite motionless. Clearly this stuff was stronger than we had imagined possible. Unfortunately, though, Gurt was naturally curious as to why I had opened the door of her hut; so, blocking with my body the sight of Parra's huddled form, I ushered myself within, rubbing my hands and making remarks about ensuring that she was comfortable.

'Well, and indeed I am, young gentleman,' she said, 'and I bet that you're a one that all the girls would like a tumble with.' While saying this she made curiously revolting gestures which were patently designed to inflame my passions. 'If you wait 'til tomorrow when the unicorn's been killed, I'll gladly welcome your galleon into safe anchorage myself.'

'Gosh, that's decent of you!' I said, pretending enthusiasm.

'Come here, handsome mannikin, and sit by me for a while,' she said, gesturing towards a crude couch and a flagon of wine. 'It's been lonely here these last few hours.'

I was in something of a quandary. If I dropped the remaining speck of Seth's horn into her flagon, there was a good chance that she would expect me to drink from it first. This would make my approaching task tolerable, except that there was the risk that it might kill me, as it had seemed to kill Parra. On the other hand, if she were the first to drink from the flask, I could expect her to attempt to rape me with inhuman zeal – a prospect which did not appeal to me much, especially since I didn't care to think about what she would do in her frenzy should she fail in her task. Ideally, of course, I could have arranged things so that we each sipped simultaneously, but there were no goblets in sight.

Gurt extracted me from my dilemma herself. 'You'd better not drink anything, young man,' she said greedily, clutching the flagon to her scrawny bosom. 'I don't want you to fall asleep while you're supposed to be guarding me.'

'Can't I just have a sniff?' I pleaded. 'It really is bloody cold out there.'

'Well, all right,' she conceded, 'but no drinking any.' She hawked into the flagon just in case I should be tempted, then passed it over to me. Distracting her attention for long enough to slip in the speck of horn was easy enough, and soon she once more had the flagon cradled in her long arms.

'Take a drink yourself,' I said, with more courage than I can normally muster.

'I don't mind if I do, you luscious fellow,' she said, and she raised the flagon to her lips . . .

When I recovered consciousness the village of the Hax was in uproar. I could hear Gurt's impassioned cackles above the noise of screaming and male flight. As for myself, every iota of my body seemed to have been bruised: I shuddered thankfully, grateful for the fact that I had not the slightest recollection of how those bruises had got there. I hauled myself to my hands and knees, and began to crawl off towards the edge of the forest . . .

It was not until some while later, when I had more or less recovered and when we were far from the village of the Hax, that I made a confession to Seth (I still haven't had the courage to tell Alla). 'You must stop thanking me for saving your life,' I thought.

'But why? You did.'

'I don't think so,' I thought, shifting myself uncomfortably on his back and scratching my groin for the thousandth time that morning. 'I have every reason to believe that Gurt was no danger to you at all . . .'

A young American writer who has been making a name for himself in numerous fantasy magazines and original anthologies, Steve Rasnic Tem lives in Denver, Colorado, and his story provides us with a rare example of the use of American Indian myths in fantasy literature.

When Coyote Takes Back The World

Steve Rasnic Tem

It was two days before the fire wind came that my brother Long Tom, he with the cancer and little time left for talking, he who laughed where I spent most of my days sadly, drew down the serious face over his entire body and said, 'Coyote is taking back the world, brother.'

Then he was silent a time, and would not go to the local game hall, or drink beer with me in the old white man's place down on 43rd Avenue. Nothing I said cheered him, my dying brother, and so we sat together a while thinking about this, letting ourselves return to that childhood where we stalked old washing machines and junked autos in the Oklahoma backwoods, and each day we danced in the dust or swam through seas of blue stem grass. The traffic roar faded into mumblings and the night floated up over our hotel window before my brother spoke again.

'It is time we told our friends, brother.'

So I went with my brother down into the city streets, as I had many times before. I did not question how he knew this thing, for my brother has known many things before they happened. And although he has been laughed at by both the whites and our own people, I have kept my speech to myself, and followed him.

Even as a child, from the first day I jumped down from my mother's womb, I followed my older brother in everything. I played where he wanted to play; I was angry when he was angry. I remember the day our mother found us playing in one of the ancient dry wallows of the vanished buffalo – my brother liked to think their ghosts still grazed there – she was crying and telling us our grandfather had died and that we were to come home. My brother had been sullen and I tried my best to beat him in sullenness. It was a trait given him by our grandfather, I think; our grandfather was a bitter man. He had lost much to the white man; our family's rich river-bottom land had gone to the mixed blood during the Oklahoma allotment. Over the years he had been reduced to doing seasonal work helping the white farmers – strawberries in May, beans in July, cotton in August and September – spending money as fast as he could make it on cars, washing machines and whisky. For a while he was a fishing guide at one of the lake resorts, a resort built on stolen Indian land.

My brother Long Tom said grandfather was really a member of the Keetoowah Society, the Nighthawks, the secret club that defied the whites and kept the old ways alive. And I tried to believe this, although I could not remember grandfather ever leaving the house for any meetings.

After he died the Indian agent took our land for another resort. He said there was a paper grandfather had signed, but I never saw it.

As my brother and I entered the city streets – the poor, run-down ones by the park – I could see there were many people walking. Everyone seemed to have left his house, his apartments. Some were gathered around front verandahs with radios. The wars in the east had reached a high-pitched madness. There were troubles with the sun. Earthquakes had levelled cities in this country and in other places. Such things had been happening for months, until it seemed everything was falling apart. Everyone seemed to have a favourite theme for the end of the world. With everything collapsing, ending, every doomsayer suddenly seemed prophetic. My brother had Coyote.

First my brother lead us to the city park, where old Indians sat beneath the trees and drank cheap wine and talked about many things, many Indian things they knew in their younger days, and for some, many Indian things they had heard about but never seen. Old Hickorytooth was there, his yellowed skin slick with sweat. My brother stood over him a long time before Hickorytooth showed one tobacco-coloured eye.

'Hey, Long Tom,' Hickorytooth whispered, and I noticed new teeth had been broken.

'Hey, Hickory,' I replied, since my brother wasn't saying anything.

Hickorytooth closed his eye and soon I could hear him growling in his sleep. Then the tobacco eye opened again and turned up like a dead fish eye. 'Tom?' he said again, and I knew he had decided we were there, and he was scared.

'Coyote, Hickory,' my brother said. 'He's coming back for it.'

'Coming back . . .' Hickory said to his feet.

'Coming back for the world, Hickory,' my brother said.

Hickorytooth nodded his head solemnly. My brother turned, and I followed.

My brother Long Tom looked like I imagined the Old Ones, like the ancient Cherokee warriors, Oconoslota, Doublehead, John Watts – straight black hair to his shoulders, high cheeks and wiry build. He used his hands when he talked, laughing at his own jokes in the Indian way. But he laughed little now. Some Indians say cancer is a white man's disease – I don't know. But it changed my brother; in his face I could see that the Ravenmockers were plucking at him, sucking away his remaining years, his skin losing its colour and growing so thin I thought I might see through it some day, so that to me he began to resemble one of the dreamed-of Nunnehi, the sacred people.

The park animals, the pigeons and the squirrels, kept to the edges of the paths this day. Squirrel climbed out on a branch and hailed us with his green eyes.

'They know,' my brother said. 'They wait for us to vanish. Coyote's coming; they prepare a welcome.' Still, my brother did not smile, and I missed the smile of my brother.

I was frightened. This look of my brother's made me believe what he said was true. I began to repeat some of my grandfather's old chants silently to myself. Now! In front of me Uk'ten' will be going, spewing flames. Now! In front of me the Red Mountain Lion will be going, his alert head reared. Nothing can harm me! I am dressed as well as the Redbird! I am as manly! I can do as much!

We walked for some time in the park, my brother not speaking to me, I continuing to follow like some dog. I thought he must be seeking Martin, the Old One. But Martin was not to be seen here, I thought. In the old white man's bar, I thought, but I could not say this to my brother.

I tried to think about when we were boys in Oklahoma together, taking the park, trees and shrubs and all, back to that time. It made me feel better. Flinty hillsides and narrow back roads; pine, hickory and cypress woods, pecan trees; the heat of the day so bad and then the cold at night, drought then flood – the seasons fighting their little wars; long snakes of trees marking the river-beds; bright blue-painted sky, rich cinnamon clay; blue stem grass in the spring so thick and slow-moving, light green with the wind, dark green against it, reddish-brown in summer, purple and copper in fall. In storms the air so full of sparks the horns of the cattle would glow. Small birds juggled like balls in the roaring wind. Grandfather used to say not to worry if you lost your hat; you could always grab the next one blowing by.

There would be no more such times. Grandfather was dead with the old stories, the old life. All that was left for me of the tribe, the Lost Cherokees in the stories, had been passed into my brother. Only his tongue could spell for me the right words, the secret names of my people's dreams. I knew no one else. But Long Tom, oh my only brother, was dying.

We used to play spaceman and alien, cops and robbers. One day I wanted to be cowboy against his Indian and he cracked my head with a stone. Silly, I sometimes thought. We Cherokee were cheated, killed, decimated on The Trail Where They Cried, our culture virtually wiped out in courtrooms and legislatures after that. But what does that mean now? Who could continue to be angry about such things, such a long time ago? You complain so much, how terrible it is – *A-sga'-si-ti!* Mean! – you complain again and again until you begin to sound comical, even to yourself. You begin laughing about yourself, and then crying, for the past cannot be changed. You can hate yourself that way.

The hatred there – the whites had no right! – it makes you sick. For a long time after my grandfather's death and we had been forced to leave the farm – my mother drinking herself to death, my father leaving for new work in Denver and never coming back – I had those violent, shameful dreams. The world blew apart because I wished it so. People were dying, smoking and burning. The great dragon Uk'ten' from our Cherokee legends circled the world and made it disappear piece by piece, city by city with his terrible breath. Soon only Uk'ten' was left, smiling his reptile smile. And I'm ashamed to say I was glad. In my dream I was glad.

My brother Long Tom had never made any secret of his bitterness. He would never forgive. I used to think he must be pretending, that his imagination had got the better of him – how could he feel such bitterness? But my brother was honest; he wore his dreams on his face.

The wind had come suddenly warm and I was chilled by it.

My brother stopped and turned into the trees bordering our path. He approached one gnarled, ancient oak and stopped before it. Then he walked around the tree. Martin was leaned up against the other side, sleeping.

Martin opened his eyes and looked past my brother. He was an old man, his white hair, his pale, disappearing face lined with stories – already half-ghost I thought, already on his way to the Other Side Camp. He spoke like a wind breaking ice in ponds I remembered. I was eight, and had been frightened of the sound. Like bones breaking, it had seemed. The dead ones singing how lonely they are, and wanting your company.

'Coyote . . .' my brother said.

'I know this,' Martin replied. 'He is finally coming. He will be with us again.'

'He will take it all back.'

'But it is his,' Martin said. 'It is his to take. He made it from the bit of mud the grebe gave him. He spread it around over the sea and made the earth. He heard the wolf and the wolf came to be. He made the Indians and spread them around so they would be in many places. He picked up the medicine stones and they became buffalo. It is his right; these things are his to take back.'

'I know these things,' my brother said, and I heard some anger in his voice. 'We must be ready. The animal people are ready. So we must be ready.'

'And the Strange Ones? The other Old Ones?' Martin said softly.

'Coyote will cast them out. He has told me of this.'

I stared at my brother. For a time I stared as the two men talked, not understanding what they were saying. My brother did not seem simply my brother then.

We left Martin and started back across the park. I had no idea where we were going, but I was content to follow.

'The Strangers, the other Old Ones ... who are they, brother?' I asked him.

My brother smiled for the first time that day. 'Some say they are what is left of the Old Animal People, the giant animal people, who took on the disguise of the human beings a long time ago. Others think they are magicians from some other place ...'

'Aliens? You mean people from other worlds?'

Long Tom shrugged. 'I do not know. It does not matter. They will be unimportant in the end.'

'But they ... change?' I said, feeling suddenly agitated, watched. I looked back into the woods we had just left.

'We all change; we are all shape-shifters,' he said, and would not answer any more of my questions.

But I remembered a time when I was ten. We both were begging in restaurants and bars for food and money; we never seemed to have enough. My brother pointed an old man out to me one day in a bar. The man had very dark eyes, and greyish skin – as if he had been very sick for a long time, as if his guts were all twisted up and infected inside him. 'That one ...' my brother said, 'is Snake.' And I looked again at the man, and I *could see* the snakeness of him, the reptile. I tried not to think of it. 'He's not a good one,' my brother said. 'But maybe he's closer to Indian than these whites are.' The coldness in my brother's voice scared me badly. There were beings in the world not human. I wanted to know more, but could not bring myself to ask.

'Coyote comes ...' my brother whispered to some old Indians on their front steps. Most of them laughed and made fun of my brother, but a few nodded quietly.

The wind was warmer still, and I felt as if my thoughts were smoking. Long Tom walked barefoot on the hot pavement, steadily, with no apparent discomfort.

My brother walked into the old white man's bar. And I followed. Looking everywhere for the human beings who were not really human beings, but Strangers, Old Ones, aliens ... stumbling over my own feet looking. Yet still I followed him into the bar, wondering what would happen next.

'Coyote is coming to take back the world,' he said once he reached the centre of the room. He said it loudly, for all to hear.

The white men stared at him. A few of the Indians laughed. The old white man who ran the bar continued to wipe off the counter with a heavy scowl burnt into his face. He wore a white apron. His arms were large.

'Coyote is coming,' my brother said, and one of the young Indians spat. A steelworker. Like many Indians – dancing like foxes on the high perches – a steelworker for the white man. He stood up and walked over to my brother, and looked him in the eyes.

'You're drunk, Indian,' he told my brother. 'Why do you talk about Coyote? Old women tell of Coyote. Why do you talk about that mangy old dog?'

'Coyote made this world,' my brother said. 'He took mud from the grebe's beak after all the other ducks had failed. He spread it over the waters with his feet. He discovered wolf there, and buffalo. He found a star person who became tobacco. He created the human beings. This all belongs to him.'

The Indian smiled. 'Crazy Indian,' he said. 'Did he make the bombs they're dropping over in Russia? Did he heat up the sun? Did he shake his arse and make the earthquakes? Crazy Indian ... we don't need Coyote to do these things. We do them ourselves.'

Long Tom walked to the bar and stood facing the old white bartender. 'The Old Man Above, Yo-he-wah, made Coyote disappear. No one knows where. Coyote killed the evil spirits and the monsters and did many other things, but when he finished the Old Man made him disappear. No one knows where. Then when earthwoman is old, they say, Old Man and Coyote will come back and change things, take back what they have given.' Several men laughed but Long Tom ignored them. 'When they come all the dead will walk with them; they will leave the Other Side Camp. Earthwoman will become as she was before.

'We have waited for Coyote a long time now. But the waiting will soon end.'

'I don't serve no drunk Indians,' the old white bartender said. 'Get outta my place.'

Then my brother did a strange thing. He began to laugh.

I was frightened. After such a long time, to see laughter splitting his face, his face like a hard, sun-dried melon, splitting into smiles, chuckles, horse laughter, my brother slapping his knees and doubling over. The men in the bar stared at him. Then one by one they began to rise.

Long Tom turned to them and continued to laugh. He slapped them with his laughter; he lashed them. He heated their faces and blisters began to form at their lips and around their eyes.

The white man's bar where my brother and I had drunk beer night after night in the city summers fell down, somersaulting into the street, lifting up its arms in pleading to the sun. And all the other old buildings in the street – the boarding house hiding the ghosts of the old white miners, the ancient whorehouse now a drugstore on the corner, the place where the Chinamen were killed – all of them fell to their knees and shook out their hair wailing at the skies.

And the sky flipped over and dragged its tongue down the street.

And the trees climbed out of their holes and leaped at the people.

And I moaned in fear and despair as my brother held me.

And when my brother and I climbed out of the broken arms of the old white man's bar, we were alone, and earthwoman had pulled up her nightdress to cover the broken faces of the city.

There were balls of fire in the dark eyes and mouths of the city. There was emptiness in the streets.

'The white men?' I asked my brother softly.

'Coyote has covered them with their fancy clothes: their towers and townhouses. He has played a good joke on them, I think. A few are left . . . he will play with them later.'

'The Strange Ones?'

'You hear them, brother.' I heard a scrabbling and a murmuring beneath the rubble.

And out of the broken-backed buildings, the crippled houses, came the dark shapes of these others, resembling the giant animal people of the old times, having left their human being suits back in the dust. But who could say what they were – aliens or the old animal people or something else? Who could tell?

A face like Raven's, his head dark and slick, his yellow beak snapping, floated by my head and around the corner where two walls cried on each other's shoulder. I drew cold up through my tattered boots and it curled into a ball inside my belly.

A tail swung above the ruins across the street, large and broad like Coyote's canoe paddle, and Beaver thundered by, slapping the street and stirring up the dust.

A giant yellow eye blinked once above my head, twice over my shoulder, and Crow spread his wings and knocked the crying walls down.

Fox ate the bricks and mortar from the pavements. Deer leaped into the pockets of fire and sang. Squirrel tumbled and played in the piles of broken glass.

And my brother laughed and laughed and laughed.

'Are these the animal people?' I asked my brother.

'Watch.' He pointed down the darkened street, where several of the animals had gathered.

Indians – some whom I knew, some whom I did not – were crawling out of the ruins and staggering to their feet. And as they walked into the street the animal people were grabbing them, striking them, and leading them to a place where they were bound. The animal people spat on them, called them dirty. They forced many of the Indians to work on a wall built out of rubble and twisted metal.

'A stockade. A camp,' my brother said beside me.

I saw Old Martin slapped by Fox, then shoved to the ground. I witnessed Hickorytooth being stabbed several times by Porcupine. He lay bleeding in the street, the animal people trampling him as they began herding their prisoners into the stockade.

'They have waited many years for this,' my brother said.

'It has happened before . . .' I said to him, looking up into his hard eyes, but he would not answer me.

The Trail Where They Cried. My grandfather never tired of telling my brother and me of the thing. Children waving good-bye to the mountains – and they used to say the rain wouldn't fall on those mountains, the Snowbirds, unless the Cherokee were there. The elderly dying in the sleet and snow – sleeping on the ground without a fire, and they had given all the blankets to the children. Twenty-two buried at each stopping place from the pneumonia, silent graves marking the trail outside Chatta-nooga, Athens, Princeton, Marion, Jackson, Springfield, Fayette-ville, the whites coming from the town to watch them move.

Families separated, driven like cattle, penned up like cattle in stockades with no shelter, having to urinate in public, losing everything save what they carried, wheels and horses and rain and endless rain, a quagmire . . .

Grandfather cried when he told of the old women with bare feet and heavy loads, a fifth of the nation lost. Graves desecrated for the silver pendants and ancestral jewellery left to the dead; the dead stripped! Many of the children never smiled after that trail, never again.

The removal, they called it.

The animal people began prodding the Indians within the stockade with claws and sharp teeth. The Indian faces: pale and stark, the eyes dead.

The principal people, we used to call ourselves. Ani-Yun-Wiya.

I looked up at my brother. His face was in shadow. A dark triangle of shadow seemed to grow from just behind his ear, spreading into his jaw, making his head seem longer, longer . . .

My brother growled in his throat and he showed his eyes to me. Large with enormous whites, dark pupils. The grey-furred snout. He sniffed me. Then licked the side of my head with a long pink, probing tongue.

My brother howled. It was pain and anger. It was Coyote.

The animal people stopped and stared. Porcupine showed his yellow eyes. Fox began to bay, Ferret to whine. I could hear Old Martin in the stockade, muttering an ancient prayer.

'My brother?' I stared into Coyote's dark eyes. 'Where are you?'

Coyote made a yapping, almost laughing sound, then drew his long muzzle back and used it to point at the night sky.

I looked up into the narrow streamer of stars stretched out over earthwoman's black shroud. The dog road, the milky way leading into the Darkening Land. Usunhiyi. And a white shape there – or did I imagine it? – of a deer. Oh my brother, Long Tom, cinnamon deer, leaping up the dog road into the Darken-ing Land.

Coyote was yapping louder, laughing harder now, and one by one the animal people began to peel away from my people in the stockade. One by one they dropped to the ground as Coyote's song became louder, Beaver then Fox then Crow then Snake, and their dark shadows, their true shapes, slipped out of the animal people suits and the Strange Ones, the aliens, blew away in the wind of Coyote's song.

He looked down at me, grinned, and licked my face.

I struggled to keep the fear in my belly. It wanted to reach out and grasp my throat. I did not want to see this thing; I was afraid. I suddenly did not want to see the ancient way come back; it was all too fearsome. I did not want Coyote to take the world back.

Coyote yapped and reared his great head. His mouth snapped and his tongue licked. Earthmother rolled over in her sleep. Dirt flew into massive mounds as the broken city dug itself a hole in terror, jumped in, and began covering itself over. Mountains rose on all sides of me. The Indians from the stockade, the last of them, Old Martin, fell into the hole with terrified shrieking. Coyote sang, and the trees jumped on top of the mountains. Coyote laughed valleys full of tears, and the tear rivers flowed into lakes and oceans. The night fell down with amazement and hid behind the mountain. New animal people came out to greet the sun Coyote had hung on the sky like an ornament. Coyote laughed and laughed and laughed, and earthwoman changed her dress and put on beads.

I turned to Coyote. 'And me?' I whispered.

Coyote frowned and looked puzzled. He looked over my shoulder and grinned his Coyote grin at what he saw. I turned slowly to see.

Old Man, Yo-he-wah, was limping down the road. He had a tree trunk helping him walk; he carried another larger tree over his shoulder. When he reached Coyote he embraced The Trickster, then rolled him up like paper and slipped him into the purse at his belt. Then he looked back down the road.

My brother Long Tom, my handsome brother Long Tom, was leading Old Martin and the others back from the Darkening Land. I ran to greet them, but suddenly Old Man was in my way.

He shoved the massive tree in the ground. He pushed me on to the first branch. He made me climb.

When I reached the top of the tree I discovered that I could see a long distance. I could see my brother and the other Indians building the fires below. I could see Moon dropping over the mountain and swimming slowly after Old Man.

I am dressed as well as the Redbird. I am as manly. I can do as much.

I remember all of this. I sit high in the branches of the tree, near the centre of the city park. The city stands up around me and makes its stomach noises. We are both shape-changers. We are all shape-changers. I wait for Coyote to knock it all down again, to break its arms and kick it into the deepest hole.

I think about my brother and I cannot sleep. I cry from yearning for him but the tears will not leave my large, clear eyes.

My name is Owl.

Since her last novel, *The Passion of New Eve* (1977), Angela Carter has devoted most of her omnivorous energies to journalism and the modernising of fairy tales. *The Bridegroom* appeared in the magazine *Bananas* in 1979 and has not been featured in any of her collections to date.

The Bridegroom

Angela Carter

This girl, archaic, two-dimensional, with stiff outlines like a figure in a woodcut at the head of a ballad, stuck resentfully in her body like a cat locked in a lumber-room.

Sometimes she would not comb her hair for days and threatened the eyes of the maids with her nail scissors when they tried to comb it for her. When these fits took her, she wouldn't wash her face nor change out of her draggled nightgown. Then she would not eat a bite for weeks on end, hurling the trays of food they brought her across the room, smash! against the wall; gaunt as famine, mad as fever, who would have guessed Lisaveta would one day inherit as much of the wild mountains that surrounded her father's castle as the eye could see?

When there was a storm, Lisaveta watched the weather from her casement for hours, tense with envy; she pinched her maids, slapped them with the flat of her hands and cried, out of rage and frustration. Fate had given her too small a theatre in which to act out passions which remained felt but perpetually inexperienced *as* passions, finding expression only as self-mortification and petulance.

At other times, she subsided in front of her mirror and scrutinised it for hours as if her appearance might offer her some clue as to her own bewildered nature. But the mirror was not prepared to tell her who she was, although its connivance assured her she possessed the visible apparatus of femininity. Then she would dig her hand into the rouge pot and plaster on a new face but she always botched the job for she had no mother to tell her what was excessive in a woman; she would appear at dinner in the baronial hall crudely overbidizened, nervously apprehensive of this other person whose face she had put on in the looking glass.

Her laughter was thin and hysterical. Her voice was now a whimper, now a growl; she was half dying of boredom. Her face was far too full of bones. Her restless fingers teased her skirts into pleats or tore a lace handkerchief to shreds. Her eyes glittered too much, she coughed dryly, like a sheep; hadn't her mother died of consumption? It was high time Lisaveta married; if she were not married soon, she might die and then there would be nothing to bargain with.

So her father, the count, careful of his acres as he was of his moustaches, offered his heiress for sale to the highest bidder. Whoever bought Lisaveta would one day own innumerable well-forested acres, home of the wild boar, deer and eagle, with all the titles that went with them. A marriage was arranged immediately; the castle prepared for the wedding. There was a great cooking, sweeping and dusting and a consignment of French seamstresses appeared from the capital to fit Lisaveta for her trousseau. But Lisaveta cried and sulked in her room and nothing would console her.

Her bridegroom's lands and titles, joined with her father's, would give the son of their marriage a principality to play with. They told her her bridegroom had a mild temper, a soft voice, and a particular fondness for music, painting in water-colour and botany. Nevertheless, from his bride's point of view, he had one great fault; he suffered from a hereditary affliction of the skin, a kind of leprosy, that covered him all over with a net of white scales from the crown of his head to the back of his heels so, in public he always covered his face with a supple mask of very soft kid, tinted a lifelike pink. This mask, they said, was so ingenious you could hardly tell the difference. They told Lisaveta the mask made his condition almost undetectable and, anyway, she would soon grow used to it but she would not be consoled; now she cried every day and starved herself to a stick.

However, Lisaveta could sulk as much as she liked; nothing could stop the wedding. Sometimes, when she stared at her mirror or her heart lifted at the sound of thunder, she might have been visited by an intimation she would grow up to be a woman; but in fact, she was only an appendage to her husband's property and those in charge of her treated her with the indifference of the weather.

The groom set out for his wedding in a fur-covered palanquin suspended from a pole between the brawny shoulders of a brace of serfs. They boxed him up like candy; he lolled on satin cushions sniffing a pomander to relieve his nostrils of the stench of his own rotting flesh. A dwarf was tucked in among his coverlets to entertain him and crates of delicious food followed him on pack-horses to pleasure his fastidious palate en route.

A band of horsemen rode with him to afford him protection against the brigands who infested the forests but they could not protect him from the storm.

A deluge engulfed the track between the forest pines down which they travelled; horses and riders were swept away. The palanquin was hollow as a boat and floated but the poor dwarf in terror abandoned his master, scrambled out and drowned. The groom sat tight; he sat the storm out because he was paralysed with fright and when his little ark beached safely on dry ground, he was too timorous to peek out to see where the storm had brought him so he stayed snug indoors, listening to the thunder echo among the peaks and the rain drum on his roof, twittering to himself, and, to soothe his nerves, munching marrons glâcés from an air-tight box that the water had not spoiled.

He stayed there until a brigand found him. This brigand made a poor home in a cave in a ravine and dressed himself in the skins of the wild beasts he had killed. He had once also killed men; fleeing the noose Lisaveta's father ordered for him, he took to the mountains where he nourished vengeance. Solitude had softened his heart a little and, though he admired the satins and sables amongst which his dainty foundling retreated, squeaking, neverthless, he scooped up the bridegroom in his arms and took him to shelter.

The bridegroom fastidiously repulsed the broth made from rabbit and wild parsley the brigand offered him, preferring to broach a fresh box of marrons glâcés. An apparition, a fair-ground puppet with sodden finery clinging to its joints, he perched in the shadowed recesses of the brigand's cave among bones of eaten meat, an object of amazement, a soft divinity rescued from the flood just before it melted, haloed in an odour of putrefaction, nibbling sweeties. A fat diamond on his cocked little finger glittered in the light of the brigand's smoky fire. A small, pink, dainty tongue-tip came out of the slit in the mask to lick the crumbs of sugar up.

Lisaveta's eyes were mirrors for the violence of the elements;

she never left the window that the furious winds rattled. The seamstresses knelt at her feet, pinning up her white satin hem; the cooks basted sucking pig in the odorous caverns of the kitchens; her father contemplated the felicity of the alliance as his valet combed and greased his festive moustache for him; the priest was lighting the candles in the chapel. Lisaveta thought: 'I hope the storm will kill the bridegroom.'

Though the storm spared him, the brigand decided to accomplish what the elements had left undone. When he heard of the bridegroom's destination, he stabbed him with his hunting knife, stripped him naked and donned the mask and garments of the other.

The wind and rain died down. Through a morning as delicate as a convalescent, the brigand, in no way distinguishable from what he was not, made his way across the mountains to the count's castle on foot, equipped with a story of disaster and an irrefutable alias. The draggled relics of his retinue, limping one by one into the castle yard as the evening sun touched the turret windows, came too late for the wedding; on the dais, presiding over the feast, sat the groom and his bride.

Lisaveta's hair stood up in spikes and the wild abstraction of a woman's face was painted on her own. Now that she was signed, sealed and delivered over to her husband, she experienced to the full her own impotence. She was not a bride, she was a territorial asset. Her satin dress clothed her, she did not wear it; it scarcely seemed to belong to the living skeleton inside it. Her eyes went this way and that way around the hall as if she were searching for a way out. When the bridegroom, studded with jewels, an artificial man, a prince of dolls, accidentally brushed against her, she shuddered. Anger and resentment stopped her tongue; she could not speak.

Then, by torchlight, with all the impedimenta of Nordic romanticism, she was escorted to bed amidst a coarse innuendo of horns and kettledrums. The maids laid her out in an extravagance of artificial lace. They saw her pitiful trepidation but remembered her rages; there was not one of them that did not think, spitefully: '*Now* she'll get what's coming to her.' Draughts wandered behind the tapestries. The candle flames dipped hither and thither so the shadows swelled and lurched.

The hangings on the bed swelled and billowed as Lisaveta waited between clean sheets for the embrace that would set the seal on the contract.

At the soft thud of his fist on the door, her maids curtseyed out backwards and in he came, dressed for the occasion in a long, cambric nightshirt his father-in-law had worn on his own wedding night and now lent to him because the bridegroom had no baggage of his own. The mask concealed his face and she thought he was the leper.

He approached his flinching bride as delicately as he would have stepped up to a fanged beast in a trap. Her balked energies pelted him with pillows, candlesticks, even the piss-pot from under the bed. But, although the outlaw knew perfectly well she was not a woman at all, only the key to the lands beyond the window, he took advantage of her woman's shape and his own greater strength and raped her. There was no pleasure in it for him, either; rather, a grim satisfaction that, one day, he would sit in the place of the man who once sat in judgment on him and whose daughter would bear his own children. He abused her until the cockerels announced the approach of dawn when, secure behind his mask, he slept. Lisaveta sobbed and bled while the ghostly light of day entered the disordered room.

She thought how the embossed veil of scabs beneath his nightshirt was her own wedding veil; but the fine fabric of his nightclothes had denied her the knowledge of the perfect corruption of his body, which would make of her own physicality a living denial of flesh she only knew she possessed by the pain it caused her. She raised herself on her elbow and looked down at her violator; that she would become as he was now impelled her to stretch out towards his mask.

The bridegroom woke to see her eyes of wonder. He knew, in the moment she had snatched off his mask, he had fallen entirely under the protection of her mercy; he shook her until her teeth rattled, held a knife against her throat and told her he would kill her unless she kept her mouth shut.

Now Lisaveta found herself, not the instrument of her father's ambition but that of a stranger's revenge. Enclosed within his mask, the bridegroom came down to breakfast with his hand clapped tight around the wrist of his ashen-faced bride, who carried her secret with as much terror as if it were the first of her children.

When her husband went out hunting with her father, the count was carried home on a barn door with a broken neck and Lisaveta came into her inheritance, although it passed through her as if she were a shadow and her husband the only being with substance. If her status had changed, it still remained contingent. However, she herself changed; she grew silent. She no longer tormented the maids so that now they giggled: 'The taming of the shrew!' She stopped painting her face altogether, she was scared of seeing herself in the glass.

But, though the real bridegroom had been left for dead, he was not. Highland villagers taking their pigs to root for acorns discovered him where he had dragged himself to the mouth of the cave, bleeding from the wound in his chest. When they saw the nacreous web on his face, they thought it was a sign he had dropped from heaven, took him back to their village and cared for him with rough kindliness until he was well enough to tell them what had happened to him. The count's tenants had circulated many rumours amongst themselves about the leper-bridegroom and, when they saw his scabs, they believed his story. They shrouded him in home-spun that chafed his skin, loaded him on a pony that he sat like a sack of potatoes and took him off to the castle.

The guards laughed at him and the children of the servants pelted him with stones and dung but he made such a fuss that at last they let him ride his pony into the hall because they thought he was a poor fool who would provide the new count with a little diversion after he had finished his dinner. But the leper was impervious to their jeers although he was taken aback to see his former self seated proud as you please upon the dais, tearing meat apart with gloved, jewelled fingers and throwing the bones to the dogs while the gaunt, pale woman beside him broke her bread but did not eat it.

When the deposed bridegroom saw the nature of the masquerade, he cried out angrily.

With a contemptuous air of disbelief his chief defence, the impostor allowed him to tell his story and, his thin voice stuttering and breaking, accuse milord of attempted murder and fraudulent impersonation. But milord was shaking in his borrowed shoes for only the mask protected him from discovery. Lisaveta had only to tear it away and he was a dead man.

When Lisaveta saw she was the arbiter of destiny, she tasted power for the first time in her life. She was the mediator between the whining wretch in his coarse wrapper and the killer who sat beside her. She, he and the leper were the only beings in the whole world who knew the face beneath the pink kid mask. She looked from one to the other of them and thought of justice, but only briefly; she thought of her dead father and only remembered his moustaches. She thought of her own face in the mirror but then she felt despair for she could not rely on her own judgment for she did not know who she was.

The man she had married fixed a stern eye on the table in front of him for he knew, if he were to betray the slightest weakness, he would be lost; he understood the nature of wild animals. But the other demanded restitution imperiously, with the arrogance of his rank; he was sure he must be believed. Lisaveta heard him demand her as though she was his by right but the murderer said nothing. Then there was silence.

Lisaveta, for just as long as the silence lasted, was, for the only time in her life, a being capable of choice.

'Her father gave her to me,' said the leper, to clinch the matter. 'I am to inherit everything.'

Lisaveta threw back her head and laughed. She put on a fine show of a light heart; and, at that moment, her heart was indeed light, as she escaped his intransigence.

'Don't I know my own husband?' she said. 'Doesn't he sit beside me? And this is the village idiot with a rash on his face!'

As soon as she had spoken, her life was over. She was the only one who could confirm the outlaw was the leper and now, by saying such a thing was so, it became so. He turned into the leper and, immediately, she ceased to be his destiny. She reverted again to two dimensions. She was an inconvenient thing again. She had lived for only as long as the silence in which she chose whose victim she would be. Freedom had betrayed her. Yet what else could she have done? The only liberty she possessed was that of choosing her master. She did not understand that; but she knew she had been most grossly duped and relapsed into an uneasy silence.

They took the leper outside, put him in a barrel stuck with nails on the inside and rolled him down a hillside, according to the penalty for fraud practised in that country. While the impostor and Lisaveta lived together for the rest of their lives.

Protean Brian Aldiss is at ease in all genres, from SF to mainstream, autobiographical, comic or fantasy fiction. His latest success has been the first volume of the planned Helliconia trilogy *Helliconia Spring*. His tale is the first of several stories from Helliconia which can't find a place in the actual novels and offer a fascinating glimpse at his imaginary world.

The Girl Who Sang

Brian Aldiss

Mochtar Ivring peered over the flowers on his balcony and saw in the street below a beautiful girl, singing. It was the sound of her voice which had brought him to the balcony.

Most of the street lay in shadow, but the girl's head and torso were in sun. Her dark glossy hair shone, her cheeks shone. When she glanced up at him, green eyes dazzled for a moment in the early light. On her arm she carried a basket. She disappeared into a house, taking with her all the magic from the scene.

Craning to catch the last glimpse of her heel, Mochtar heard his landlady from the room behind say, 'Mind my jessikla plants, now!' He returned into his room where Mrs Bornzam was clearing his modest breakfast and making his bed.

'Beautiful singing,' he said, explaining away his supposed threat to her window-boxes.

'That's the girl who sings.' Mrs Bornzam said, with her customary air of setting in its place all that was known about the world.

The singing and the sight of the girl had momentarily lifted Mochtar's spirits, though they sank again when he contemplated the grey-clad bulk of Mrs Bornzam. The city of Matrassyl was stocked with people like Mrs Bornzam, all fat and corseted and dull and ungenerous of spirit. He had been here far too long, but was too poor to afford to leave. So he lodged with the Bornzams in the back street, and advertised in their front parlour window for pupils. At present, the number of his pupils was precisely one. The war. Everything could be blamed on the war.

Although he had all day to kill as usual, Mochtar left the house in some haste, pulling on his yellow coat as he went, buttoning up its fur collar, as he hurried into the street. Not only did he wish to avoid Mrs Bornzam's conversation which had for its *leitmotif* the contemptible inability of teachers to earn good money, but he wanted to catch another glimpse, if possible, of the girl who sang.

The street was full of Matrassylans trudging to work. They were a dumpy race with a preference for grey cloth. Mochtar raised his eyes to the distant hills, but no one else looked. When he came into a grander thoroughfare, men on horseback mingled with the crowd of pedestrians, and a cabriolet laboured slowly up to the castle, the driver lashing his horses. On the corner of this thoroughfare and the street where the Bornzams lived stood a tavern. As he paused there, the girl who sang left by one of its side doors.

The way she swung her basket told him that it was now empty, and he guessed she had been delivering bread. As she paused in the sunlight, a few notes escaped her lips. Then she saw Mochtar staring and stopped, smiling, her lips apart, to give him an enquiring look.

She was more lovely than he had imagined. Her face was rather long, though this was counterbalanced by a round little nose. Her mouth looked generous, her eyebrows were arched and a trifle severe. Heavy lashes offset her light green eyes. If these features sounded miscellaneous when catalogued, when glimpsed together their effect was delightful – even breathtaking. Mochtar thought, and before he could allow shyness to overwhelm him, he had stepped forward, raised his hat, and addressed this beautiful creature.

The beautiful creature regarded him from under her lashes. With a disarming smile, she sang a few bars of a melody and then passed by, tripping daintily up the side street. Thus a chance was presented to gaze at her slender figure, in which the dumpiness of Matrassyl was nowhere apparent.

He had certainly never heard a more delectable sound than her singing. Cloddish bodies pushed by him as he stood, striving to capture her elusive tune in his head. At one moment he thought it familiar, at the next not. The harsh sounds of Matrassyl, thrown against stone walls and cliffs and echoing back, drove it from mind.

He moved on when a squad of infantry marched noisily by, and made his way to the Question Mark. The usual one-armed beggar stood outside, but Mochtar brushed past him. He favoured this coffee house because one of the waiters was friendly, hailing from the same distant country, born within sight of the same sea, as Mochtar. After greeting his friend, he retired to his usual table and abstractedly unfurled a newspaper to see how the war was going.

War had been raging for nineteen years, prowling back and forth across the continent of Campannlet like plague, springing up again when seeming exhausted. It showed no sign of reaching any conclusion, despite the oratory of statesmen.

It was the war, and the prankish accidental nature of war, which had stranded Mochtar, at the age of twenty, in Matrassyl. Innocent of all knowledge of any such city, he was studying in a university in the Qzints, when the university town had been invaded by a Pannovalan army. The invading army took over the university buildings as its headquarters. Mochtar and other students had been made prisoner and forced to work in gangs, towing barges south-eastwards for several hundred miles along the towpaths of the Ubingual Canal, which cut through the heart of the strife-locked continent. One stormy night, Mochtar had dodged the guard, crossed the canal, and escaped, to find himself after months of wandering in Matrassyl. He was too ill to go farther. Although his strength had by now returned, return to his home by the Climont sea was impossible; for that he needed money, and a cessation to the fighting in the western sector.

Sipping his free coffee, he scoured the blurred newsprint before him.

According to the latest report, the enemy in the west was at last in retreat, following the bitter winter campaign. The double-headed eagle had gained distinct ascendancy over the sun-and-sickle – although, in the east, in Mordriat, prospects were less bright. Somehow, the news brought Mochtar little joy, certainly not enough to dislodge the girl's tune from his head. The words ... The words of the tune ... Suddenly, he resolved a part of the puzzle. He slapped his hand on the table, rattling his cup. The girl – he should have realised as much earlier – was not singing in Olonets, the local language. She sang in Slachs, an eastern language with which Mochtar was only slightly familiar.

The friendly waiter ceased his favourite occupation of staring over the green curtain into the street, and said, mistaking Mochtar's gesture, 'The news is gratifying, yes?'

'Very gratifying. We'll be home some time, and away from this prison of a town.'

'This is the day you go to teach your lame boy?'

'Yes. He's now my only pupil, and he's a fool. Hence my failing finances.'

The waiter nodded and bent closer. 'Listen, I have a titbit for you. A fellow told me yesterday that the duke's language teacher has gone for a soldier, silly ass, to try and find his brother lost in the eastern war against the Kzaan of Mordriat.

'The duke's enlightened about foreigners, they say. Why don't you go up to the castle and try your luck?'

'I'd never dare.'

'It couldn't do any harm. Try your luck, I say, or you may be forced to take up a waiting job too. Better to teach the surly Matrassylans than serve them, I say ... Have another cup of coffee before you leave.'

The next morning was positively springlike. When the sun Freyr rose high enough above the shoulders of the Cosgatt Mountains to shine upon the domes of the city's churches, Mochtar was already dressed and breakfasted.

Mrs Bornzam disapproved of this departure from routine as gravely as she disapproved of lateness, and expressed her displeasure by hissing through her false teeth, but her lodger escaped without delay into the street. He walked slowly up it, up to the top. It was a direction in which he rarely ventured, for the alleys became narrow and steep, and the people increasingly xenophobic. Dehorned phagors lurked in slavery here. He observed that a water-pump was being repaired. Cobbles had been taken up, a spring gushed down an adjacent way from a broken pipe, bubbling across the street.

Blessed water, he thought, which has diverted the girl who sang from her customary path towards my irresistible clutches.

As he stood where the ways met, his initiative was rewarded. Echoing among the shadowy alleys came a haunting song, and in a moment the dark girl was in sight, her basket over her arm. Her step was firm. She was as trim a vision as he had ever set eyes on.

Immediately, his hatred of the city left him. According to

legend, Matrassyl had once been the capital of an empire; now it was a dull provincial town. But the beauty of the girl who sang transformed it into a miraculous place.

He raised his hat as she approached.

'May I walk with you on your way?'

She smiled with a reserve which Mochtar felt he already knew by heart. A fragment of song drifted from her red lips. Prepared for the foreign language, he thought he grasped its simple meaning: 'I care for nobody, for nobody cares for me.'

She gave no other answer. He had the benefit of her profile along most of the street. At the door of the tavern, she turned her eyes towards him and sang a few pure notes. Then she went inside.

He waited with a light heart until she emerged with a light basket. It was puzzling: the girl who sang attempted neither to evade nor to address him. Pretty and pleasant though she was, there was something withdrawn in her manner, something which made him feel it would be impertinent to return up the street with her.

'May I see you tomorrow?' he asked. He thought, if I don't see her, the sun will not shine.

When she sang, he recognised the Slachs word for 'tomorrow', but could not understand the rest of it. That vexed him, but he went on his way rejoicing in the memory of her parting smile. What a strange, what a marvellous girl . . . And not from these parts, praise be . . . Perhaps unhuman blood ran in her veins – the blood of the Madis, let's say. Before he knew it, he had climbed the hill and was at the Anganal Gate of the castle.

The dukes of Matrassyl had seen grand times, but misfortunes of war had reduced their pomp. Mochtar was shown into a room with an unlit stove where the curtains, funereal at long windows, had moth holes in them. He sat on a side-chair, contemplating a portrait of the emperor, above which hung a tattered flag bearing the double-headed eagle, the birds of Oldorando-Borlien. Clutching his hat, he thought how the world was loaded against the young; even the expression about the emperor's whiskers proclaimed as much. You had to fight back as best you could.

When a withered clerk entered the room, Mochtar stood up.

The clerk asked him a few questions. After another wait, he was shown into the presence of the duke.

The duke sat at a polished table. He wore a green velvet jacket with lace cuffs. And a wig. Apart from a large ruby ring on one finger, and a melancholy expression, he appeared much like any ordinary human being in middle life. Unsmilingly, he motioned Mochtar to sit on the opposite side of the table, so that they could both study the other's reflection in the polished table-top.

'I have three children. I wish them to be taught Ponpt, which I understand is your native language, to a standard where they can speak it fluently and read its great works of religious literature with ease.'

'Yes, your grace.'

'The times are ill, M. Ivring, and will remain so until the forces of the sun-and-sickle are defeated. Because of the confounded war, I wish also to have my children coached in the barbarous eastern tongue of Slachdom. You have no command of Slachs, I assume?'

Caught between a wish to be honest and a wish to secure the job, Mochtar paused. Then, rather to his own surprise, he sang in his light tenor voice, in Slachs, 'I care for nobody, for nobody cares for me.'

The duke was impressed. He screwed a monocle into his left eye and surveyed Mochtar carefully.

'You are engaged, sir. My clerk will furnish you with details of salary and so forth. Before you go, outline for me your philosophy of life.'

In the midst of the paralysis which this question induced, Mochtar thought that very likely dukes were trained to freeze the air about them; it went with their exalted station in life. He recalled his pleasant home-city by the western sea, where the gulls cried; he thought of the desolate plains and mountains within which Matrassyl was ensconced; he thought of the yet more desolate lands to the east, the lands which led ultimately to the High Nktryhk, from whence, mysteriously, a girl who sang had come, emerging from clouds of war. And he thought of saying to the duke, There is no philosophy, only geography; Helliconia is a function, and humanity a part of that function. But that might not meet the case at all.

'I believe in rationality, your grace. That people should conduct their lives without superstition ...'

'It sounds commendable enough. How do you define superstition?'

'Well, your grace, we should trust to the evidence of the intellect. I can believe in this table because I can see it; yesterday, if challenged on the point, I would have been within my rights not to have believed in it, because my senses had not informed me of its existence. Hearsay evidence would not have been sufficient.'

The duke's hand went to an elaborate inkstand and played with it, seemingly without permission from the duke, who sat stiffly upright.

'You chose a trivial example upon which to suppose yourself questioned. Let us say the interrogation concerned not a piece of furniture but Almighty Akhanaba, who elects not to show himself to us. What then?'

'From this day on, I shall believe in your table, your grace, because I have witnessed its existence, and could if necessary give some account of it.'

The duke rose and pulled the bell-cord. 'Be sure you teach your charges your language and literature, not your philosophy. I also am a rationalist – but one evidently of larger capacity than you. I believe in this table as evidence of God Almighty as well as mere evidence of itself. As I see my reflection in it, so I see His.'

'Yes, your grace.'

As the dry clerk returned to escort Mochtar out, the duke said, 'Undiluted rationality leads to death of the spirit. You sing. Remember that songs are frequently more to be trusted above prose, and metaphor above so-called reality.'

From that day on, Mochtar's affairs prospered. He saw more of the girl who sang – and not only in the mornings but in the evenings and on her free afternoons. He put one or two rivals to flight. Discovering more about her became one with the advance of spring, which grew greener every day although Helliconia was entering the autumn of another Great Year. They walked in the daisy-starred meadows above the grey town, and she sang, 'Love is all lies and deception, And my lover hides in the dark wild wood.'

They sat on a fallen tree trunk, looking down at the city below, where little dumpy people moved in miniature streets. Beyond the town flowed the river, the chill Takissa. Above them, the steep meadows gave way to the harsher slopes of the Cosgatt. Somewhere up there, so rumour had it, an army flying the banners of the sun-and-sickle was approaching Matrassyl. The girl hugged her knees and sang about a house untended, where women's hearts were empty because their men were off to fight at a place called Kalitka.

Beyond the city walls, the life of the country reasserted itself. Fish flashed in the river, and a heron waited immobile for them on the bank. Butterflies and bees were at work in the scantiom nearby. Beetles glinted in the tall grass. Both suns shone. Everywhere lay double shadows, double highlights. He gestured contemptuously at the city which distance had diminished. 'Look at it – you could put it in your pocket, castle and all.'

But she had no answer for him, only her touching lament.

'Never mind Kalitka,' he said. 'What about Matrassyl and you and me? What about those highly important topics, eh?'

He grasped her impatiently, but she shook free and jumped to her feet. She looked blank, and the song died on her lips. Standing with her mouth slightly open, she presented a picture of maimed beauty.

One evening in her doorway, he kissed her lips. She put an arm about his neck and softly sang, 'Don't drive the horses too hard, coachman. There's still a long, long way to go.'

Together with the spring and their developing relationship went Mochtar's increasing involvement with the two sons and the daughter of the duke. Their ages were five, six, and eight. Though they were haughty with their language tutor, they attended to his lessons, and made steady progress in Ponpt.

Sometimes, the duchess, a thin lady in velvets, arrived at the door of the schoolroom, and listened without speaking. Sometimes the duke would appear, cramming his bulk into a small desk to attend, frowning, to what Mochtar had to say. This embarrassed his employee, all too aware of his scanty knowledge of Slachs.

Sombre though the duke's demeanour was, Mochtar detected an errant spirit under the surface; whereas her grace appeared to possess no character at all, beyond a stifled way of breathing.

'M. Irving,' said the duke, drawing him aside on one occasion, 'you may apply to the librarian, with my permission, to refer to my books. You will find there a section of volumes on Slachdom, including – if memory serves – a grammar of the Slachs tongue.'

Not since he had been forced to leave his university studies had Mochtar seen as many volumes as the library contained. The section printed in Slachs was particularly precious. It drew him nearer to the girl who sang. Here he could study her language, and make out something of the history of her race.

One afternoon, when he was sunk deep in a leather chair, reading, the duke appeared and screwed his monocle into his eye.

'You are deriving benefit from the library, my rationalist friend?'

'Yes, your grace.' Mochtar realised that this stiff-backed man, the Duke of Matrassyl – not ancient, perhaps no more ancient than twenty-eight years old, though that was ancient enough – was attempting to be friendly. Beyond closing his volume with a finger in it, Mochtar made no move to respond.

'You probably wonder how I came to have such a collection of volumes relating to Slachdom.'

Having wondered nothing of the sort, Mochtar kept silent.

The duke walked about before saying, 'I led a campaign to the east, very successful. We put the forces of the Kzaan of Mordriat to flight. A great victory, a great victory. That was ten years ago. Unfortunately, it did not end the war, and now the enemy has gathered strength again, and isn't too far from here ...' He sighed heavily.

'Anyhow, we plundered one of the strongholds of the Kzaan, and these books were part of the booty. They're decently bound, I'll give the barbarian that.'

He swung about on his heel in a military way, leaving as abruptly as he had come. Dismissing him from mind, Mochtar returned to his history of the Slachi.

The Slachi were a nation within a nation. They lived chiefly in the mountain ranges of the vast country of Mordriat, often as shepherds or brigands. They were persecuted from time to time. Many of the men were forced through poverty to join the Mordriat Kzaan's armies, where they served the sun-and-sickle loyally. Indeed, their prowess in war had enabled some exceptional Slachi to become Kzaans. Despite such occasional glories, the history of their race was one of misfortune. There had once been an independent Slachi nation, but it was over-whelmed at the battle of Kalitka ('still a subject for epic poetry', said the chronicle), six centuries previously.

As Mochtar's friendship with the girl who sang grew, so grew his knowledge of her ethnic background, and of her language.

So also did her mystery grow. She never spoke. She could not speak. She could only sing her songs. Though people in the back streets of Matrassyl knew her because of her singing, no one was her friend. None could say her name. She was the eternal foreigner.

The girl who sang worked in a bakery and lived in a garret. She had no parents, no relations, no one near her who spoke Slachs. She had no possessions, as far as Mochtar could discover – except for a long-necked binnaduria inlaid with mother-of-pearl, with which she sometimes accompanied her songs.

So beautiful was her singing that the birds of garden and meadow ceased their own warbling to listen. They would gather about her high window as they never did about the casements of those who threw them grain.

'I'm a foreigner in this town, as you are, my darling. Where were you born? Do you remember?'

'The walls of Lestanávera stand high above the stream. But life in Lestanávera is nothing but a dream,' she sang in her own tongue.

'Is that your home, Lestanávera?'

'Alas, the traitorous Vuk at night who opened up the gate, Betrayed old Lestanávera and Slachi fate.'

'Were you there then, my poor love?'

She could not reply, unless her lingering regard was a reply.

In the duke's library after lessons the next day, Mochtar found a reference to Lestanávera. It had been a great fortress on the Madavera, the main river of the vanquished kingdom of

Slachi. A traitor named Vuk Sudar had opened the gate to the Mordriat enemy and the impregnable fortress fell. Two years later came the fateful battle of Kalitka, when the Slachi nation was finally defeated, its leaders and soldiers slain.

In so many of her songs, Mochtar reflected as he walked back to his room, she made reference to events long bygone. The realisation came to him slowly that not only was song her sole means of communication: her songs were traditional, referring to events long past. The shadowy power of Lestanávera, a place he had had to look up in a book, might be either the power natural to her birthplace, or to a legend born long before her grandparents' time.

'Late again, and me standing over the pot for you,' Mrs Bornzam said, when he entered his lodgings. Mochtar took his evening meal with the senior Bornzams and their two loutish sons – a doubtful privilege. Since he was late, and politely brought up, he apologised.

'I should think so,' the lady said, in a tone implying that she found his apologies as irritating as his unpunctuality. 'Just because you work for the duke, you needn't ape the manners of the duke.'

He let his anger simmer throughout the meal, eating little despite the blandishments of old Bornzam, who was a civil enough fellow, considering that he worked in the town abattoir. He waited until after the meal, when Mrs Bornzam stacked all the dirty plates and cutlery into her sink, added her pair of china false teeth to the pile, and began the washing-up. Her teeth were always done with the dishes, and dried afterwards on the same towel, before being reinserted in her mouth.

Mochtar worked himself up to deliver something cruel, but managed only to say, 'Mrs Bornzam, I shall be leaving this house tomorrow. I will pay you till the end of the month. I refuse to eat at your table again.'

She looked round at him in horror, her cheeks turning a dull red. Fishing in the washing-up water with one hand, she brought her teeth up dripping, and pushed them into her mouth to say, 'And what's so wrong with my table, then, you little scholarly prig? You won't get better meat at any other table that's sure.'

'It's not at all sure. It's a very debatable statement. Mrs Bornzam, your temper might be better if you sang everything you had to say. You might then be less intolerable.'

'You cheeky little pipsqueak!'

'Though doubtless if you attempted to sing, your teeth would fall out. Good-night, madam.'

Feeling less triumphant next morning, Mochtar told his troubles to the girl who sang.

'Hide away your tear, Only the binnaduria sounds sweet year long.'

He kissed her passionately. 'Why can you not speak, you beauty? Yet how I love your voice. What has happened to you that the ordinary power of words has deserted you?'

What with the practice that she and his pupils gave him, he now spoke easily to her in her native tongue.

'Only the binnaduria sounds sweet year long.'

'It's not true. You also sound sweet – always.'

That word 'always' lingered in his mind as he climbed the road to the castle. To have her for always ... To take her away from grey Matrassyl, away to the sea ... But his daydreams shattered as ever on the rational rock of his having too little money. He had received a letter from his father – it had been on its way for months – but it enclosed no money for him. Damn his father, the old rogue.

Fortune, however, still smiled on him. At the close of the morning's lesson, the duke entered the schoolroom. He had a widowed cousin who also wished to learn Slachs. Would M. Ivring be her tutor for a salary she and he could agree between themselves? They expected the lady at the castle on the following day.

Mochtar had had to give up his lame pupil, the son of a burgher, in order to teach at the castle. With four pupils, his salary should be sufficient to get married on, if he could find a good room locally.

The dream changed. He would live for ever in Matrassyl with the girl who sang, and she would slowly come to speak prose like everyone else.

That evening in Freyrset he asked her to marry him. He

thought she accepted him. She sang that all the girls of the village admired the handsome young shepherd, but he had eyes for only one of the girls. She sang of a handkerchief that gleamed in the moonlight by a ruin where two young lovers had met. She sang that the river Madavera flowed by a cottage, where all who passed in boats heard a young girl singing to express her happiness. She sang, she played her guitar, she danced for him, she wept. It seemed like an acceptance.

There was no difficulty in finding a pleasant but rather expensive room in which to set up house. They consoled themselves for their extravagance by admiring the beautiful view of the river. The girl who sang knew many songs about rivers. Rivers, with ruins, broken wine glasses, soldiers, deserted lovers, lost letters, and old mothers, formed a large part of her repertoire.

The wedding ceremony presented difficulties, but Mochtar, aided by his waiter friend, found an understanding priest who agreed to join them in matrimony.

'I knew a nun with the same affliction,' the man of God observed. 'She had been raped by an enemy soldier, or perhaps it was a friendly one, and never after uttered another word. Except for her devotional singing, which was much valued in the nunnery.'

So Mochtar and the girl who sang were married, and returned in happiness to their room with a view. The bride clutched her groom, kissed him, and sang sweetly, but evaded all the usual pleasant intimacies of the bed.

It was therefore a rather gloomy Mochtar who returned to the castle to meet his new pupil. The Lady Ljubima was not the gaunt old figure in black his imagination had painted. She was a fair-haired woman of his own age, brightly dressed and flirtatious of manner. Even the duke looked more cheerful in her presence. She informed Mochtar immediately that she liked him and had no intention of mourning an old husband who had been foolish enough to get himself killed on a silly battlefield.

Standing like a statue to integrity, Mochtar informed her that while he was prepared to teach her a foreign language, he felt bound to tell her that he was newly married. She laughed, not at all put out, and named a generous sum she was prepared to pay as long as the lessons were not too dull.

Despite himself, he found himself growing to like Ljubima. She had wit, and she detested Matrassyl as cordially as he. She treated him as a slightly dim equal, and told him amusing stories of life in what she termed her 'tin-pot palace', now overrun by the hated sun-and-sickle. Their friendship progressed faster than their lessons.

When Mochtar returned to his room, there was his lovely wife, to sing to him and kiss him and cook him gorgeous meals – but not to grant him the intimacies he craved. Every day he discovered how expensive meat was, and how dusty repressed desire.

'What ails you, my love?' he asked her tenderly – he was tender to her at this time. 'What has befallen you?'

She took up her long-necked binnaduria and sang him a heartbreaking song of a lass who walked late in her garden one night, and none thereafter knew why she pined away, pined away.

He took to writing down the words of her songs that summer. She gladly helped him, singing each phrase over, her hand resting on his shoulder. At first, he did it for love, without mercenary intention. Growing more ambitious, he took music lessons in the evening with an old crone in the lower town, in order to be able to transcribe the notes of her songs into his book.

As he was walking home one evening late, Mochtar was hailed from a hansom cab. It was his fair pupil, the Lady Ljubima. She offered to drive him home, and he climbed up beside her. But she called to her driver, and they clip-clopped to her house at a great rate.

'For a glass of wine, no more!' she cried, laughing at his concern. 'Don't think I'm offering you anything else, little scholar.'

'I don't doubt that!' he said, suddenly bitter. 'Women like to lead men on – only to deny them the one thing they want.'

'Oh, la! And will you name that one thing?'

'You know what I mean – the rational end of desire.'

More sympathetically, she said, 'You speak with experience.'

'With *in*experience, more like.'

When they reached the mansion Ljubima said she was tired, she dismissed the servants and took him into her boudoir, where she poured him a glass of spiced wine. They sat companionably on a chaise longue, and Mochtar found himself pouring out the story of his strange wife. At first, he felt ashamed of his lose tongue, but a passion for declaration soon overcame him.

Silence fell when he finished.

A tear stole down Ljubima's cheek. 'Mochtar, dear Mochtar, thank you for confiding in me. Your wife sounds such a rare person. No doubt she underwent some terrible experience as a young girl – that's a tragedy. But it is obvious how much she loves and trusts you. No doubt in a year or two she will feel confident enough to grant you all you desire and more.'

'A year! A year or two! You think I can wait so long?'

She tried to calm him. He seized more wine and drank it down, flinging the glass onto the rug, where it lay without shattering.

'You must wait. Oh, yours is such a rare love! I will never do anything to sully it. Forgive me! – I admit that, on a whim, because you're amusing, I did play with the idea of a seduction scene, this being a night I am free, but now – '

He turned furiously on her.

'Played with the idea – Played with me, you mean! Just as she does. A rare love! Rare indeed! Take your clothes off, you bitch, or I swear I'll kill you.'

'I'll call the servants and have you shot. One scream is all it needs.'

He stood back. 'Ljubima, forgive me, I'm not rational. Let me stay with you tonight, I beg. I will offer no violence, only love. I'm not a violent man. Please, if you find I'm acceptable. Amuse yourself, as you intended. For myself, you know how I have grown fond of you.'

She sat. Then she raised her hands and began to unpin her hair.

'Are you sure this is what you most want?'

'Oh, yes, yes, darling Ljubima!' He fell on his knees, seizing one of her hands and kissing it. 'How can you be so sweet to me, a commoner?'

'Ask nothing – just accept,' she said. 'And don't flatter

yourself by thinking of me as nobility. I'm just a woman over-
taken by war.'

He did not pause to puzzle out her remark.

The girl who sang did not reproach her husband when he
appeared late next day. Instead, she gave voice to a slow song of
intricate rhythm, to which the refrain was, 'Oh, Marick, Marick,
are you dead, As in my dreams you were?' Smiling, she executed
a gentle dance before him. He covered his eyes.

During the next afternoon lesson, Mochtar and Ljubima were
formal. At the end of it, as they rose from the schoolroom table,
she said in a low voice, 'I accepted you last night because of the
touching story of your marriage, nothing more.'

'That is not what you said then. When may I come and see
you again?'

She looked down at the worn carpet. 'The war from the east
draws nearer Matrassyl, day by day. Who knows what will
become of us all?'

He thought that her words could have been set to music.

As she left the room, she said casually, 'You could come
tomorrow night. I'll be free then. My cab will pick you up in the
Old Square.'

Because she seemed so wealthy and he so poor, he thought,
I'm really lucky, but everything would be better if only I had
more money.

The next time the Duke of Matrassyl entered the classroom to
observe the progress his children were making, Mochtar ventured to address him.

'Your grace, your children are both brilliant and diligent at
their studies. However, they lack mastery of the correct Slachs
accent, that all-important matter, which I, not being of Slachi
origin, am unable to impart in all its nuances. May I make so
bold as to suggest that I hire for you a lady I have encountered, a
Slachi, who could come to the castle and enunciate for your
children and your Lady cousin, to their decided advantage?'

The duke regarded him from under his iron eyebrows.

'When you were first engaged, young man, my impression was
that you had little Slachs, though I grant you progressed
rapidly. Supposing this lady you have encountered . . . proves

herself a better teacher than you. Will you not then have engineered yourself out of a job?'

'This lady, your grace, speaks only her own language. She will be a perfect example but an imperfect teacher, you'll find.'

'You are still a rationalist, I perceive. Very well, bring her along.'

'She is much in demand, your grace, and not only comes somewhat expensive, but requests strongly that your grace pay her through me before she appears.'

The duke took a long look out of the window towards the mountains.

'Well, the enemy may be at the Takissa before the autumn. Before that fate befalls us, we must all enjoy life as much as we can.'

He sighed heavily. 'I have reason to believe that our old enemy, the Kzaan, will raze Matrassyl to the ground if he gets here . . . ' And he paid Mochtar the amount he demanded.

When Mochtar arrived home, he explained to his wife that she would have to sing at the castle the next day. 'Sing and dance, that will be best. We must earn some money. When the enemy gets near the gates, we are going to escape, and that requires resources. My friend in the Question Mark will come with us. Three will travel safer than two.'

Her breasts heaved beneath her blouse, and she began to sing quietly of Lestanávera, now only a ruin, where once many a handsome man and maid were seen.

'Never mind Lestanávera, my dear, let's eat supper fast, because I have to go out this evening.'

Over the pot on the stove, she hummed quietly to herself. It was the song, he recognised, about a girl who looked after her father's swine; she called to them and the swine heard her voice; but the one whom she longed to hear was dead beneath the winter's snow. He checked to make sure it was in his collection.

By now, he had over two hundred Slachs folk songs, many of them several centuries old. In the civilised capitals of the West, the collection would be worth a great deal, and his name would be made when they were published.

There was great activity as Mochtar made his way to the castle with his wife. Soldiers were marching through the streets, and a band was playing. As the band stopped, Mochtar understood the reason for the excitement. Distant cannonfire boomed in the hills. The forces of the sun-and-sickle were nearing the Takissa. He said nothing to his wife.

She sang a repertoire of songs to her audience of four, just as Mochtar demanded. To his disappointment, the duke and duchess did not appear. As they were about to leave the castle, however, the duke was standing in the hall talking to two army officers. He also was in uniform, with sword and pistol at his belt, looking formidable. A line of armed phagor guards waited motionless behind him. When he saw Mochtar, he called him over. The duke's manner was curt, his expression grim.

'I may be absent for some while. You are dismissed, Ivring. Draw what salary is owed you – my clerk will see to it – and don't come here again, ever.'

Mochtar was dumbfounded.

'But why, your grace – ?'

'You're dismissed, I said. Go.'

'But I must say good-bye to Lady – '

The duke, in turning a uniformed shoulder on him, noticed the girl who sang for the first time, and beckoned her to him. He said something to the generals, who immediately became interested.

She approached, and eyed the duke with an open curiosity in which her usual innocence protected her from fear.

'What's your name, my dark-haired beauty?'

She sang a few pure notes, 'My name is sorrow, I'm from Distack.' It was No. 82 in Mochtar's book.

One of two officers immediately took the girl by her arm, while the other officer drove Mochtar away.

'I never argue with an armed man,' he said, and fled, ignoring his wife's cries.

When he collected his fee from the duke's clerk, who would tell him nothing, he hurried from the castle. Pushing through the crowded streets, he went to cheer himself up at the Question Mark, where he gave an account of the duke's behaviour to his friend, the waiter.

'I can't understand it,' he said. 'I was the perfect teacher.'

'The war's coming this way,' said the waiter. 'Faster than expected. You're a foreigner, aren't you? Well, that's the way they treat foreigners in this rotten town. I should know.'

'Yes, you must be right. Then why did they seize my wife?'

The waiter spread his hands. It was all so obvious to him. 'Why, she's a foreigner, too, isn't she? What else can you expect in a place like Matrassyl?'

'I suppose you're right. Get me a bottle of wine, will you? What a mean way to behave to an honest chap ...'

He spent several hours drinking in the coffee house and studying the newspaper, which was full of bad news from East and West. The only item to offer encouragement was an obscure paragraph on a back page, which announced the death of a composer in his home country. Someone would have to take his place. Composers were always needed, in war as in peace. He would have to see about arranging the songs, to make them more palatable to a cultured public.

Going heavily home, he was surprised to find his room empty. His wife had not yet returned. Who would prepare his supper? Why, their bed was not even made, curse her.

Suddenly, he was angry. What pleasure had he ever enjoyed on that bed? She gave him nothing, never would. But there were others ...

His mind dwelt luxuriously on Lady Ljubima, on her beauty and ardour. Also on her way with words, always so precise, always saying exactly what she intended. A rational person, like him. Really – one had to admit it – being married to someone who could not talk or make love was misery.

He took a drink from a brandy bottle, tramping round the room, and came suddenly to a decision.

Pulling his old pack from under the bed, he stuffed some essentials into it. The bottle went in. So did the priceless folk song collection. At the door, he paused and looked round. Her long-necked binnaduria lay on the dresser. Yes, it would serve her right if he took it. At least he'd get something from her. He grabbed it.

As he walked through the streets of Matrassyl for the last time, he saw his future clear. He would be doing Ljubima a favour. He was rescuing her from certain death. Rape. Torture.

All the rest of it. This was one of the evenings she had forbidden him to see her – but what of that? Her cab was what he needed. They would escape in the cab. She would have valuables. They'd drive westward, never stopping. Never stopping till they reached the western sea. There they would live happily and prosperously, and he would be famous.

It was a long way on foot to her mansion. Double darkness had fallen by the time he arrived. As he passed under the light by the gate, he saw her holding a candle at an upper window. Ljubima saw Mochtar and waved frantically.

'She's crazy for me,' he told himself, smiling.

Her footman opened the door. He stepped into the hall. The Duke of Matrassyl emerged from Ljubima's parlour. His monocle was in his left eye. He levelled a double-barrelled pistol at Mochtar. He trembled with suppressed fury.

This apparition so astonished Mochtar that his legs began immediately to quake. He could hardly stand up, never mind speak.

'I'm glad to see you so dismayed,' said the duke, speaking in a thick voice. 'You have earned yourself a reputation as rather a cool customer. I discover you have had the infernal temerity to visit my mistress here, in the very house in which I have installed her. She has told me everything, so don't deny it.'

'But, but she – '

'You are going to be shot. I am going to shoot you. Say nothing. Pray to Akhnaba.'

Mochtar's knees collapsed. He fell sobbing to the marble tiles.

'But my poor wife. . .'

'A little late to think of her.' The duke had a grim smile on his face, as if he was enjoying these moments considerably more than Mochtar. 'Ten years ago, when fighting in the eastern campaign, one of my generals took an enemy position, and we found we had captured the family of the Great Kzaan of Mordriat – the Kzaan having fled in true Slachi fashion. My men put all the family to the bayonet, except for the Kzaan's wife and daughter, the latter scarcely seven years old. They were seized for ransom. That was a lucky day for us.'

Mochtar looked up supplicatingly, but the duke kicked him back into a crouching position.

'Both the mother and the daughter were raped on their way back here, and unfortunately the Kzaanina died. The daughter escaped from us one night. We assumed she had either died or found her way back to Mordriat. But no. You, my resourceful little trickster, found her in the back streets of this very city. Her mind's gone, but she's still of great value. The Kzaan will spare Matrassyl in order to get his daughter back alive.'

Through his snivels, Mochtar had been listening hard. He rose to his knees now, to say, 'Your grace, please believe me, I was about to hand her over. That was why I brought her to the castle, don't you see? You can't shoot the saviour of Matrassyl.'

A pleasant laugh sounded behind the duke.

'You can't shoot him, Advard. Let him go. He means no real harm – unlike the Kzaan, with whom you are prepared to deal. I wish more of your soldiers had Mochtar's nerve.'

The duke turned scowling to where Ljubima stood, tall and fair, holding before her a candle in a golden candlestick.

'You love this crawling commoner,' he said, raising the pistol.

'Oh no, no, Advard. On the contrary. He almost raped me. I'd be glad to see him go. But I hate seeing people being killed.'

Mollified by this response, the duke turned back to Mochtar. This time, something sheepish had entered into his manner.

'Listen, I shall count to ten, boy, and then I shall shoot you if you are still here. One.'

Mochtar was through the door by Three.

By Five he was back.

He smiled nervously at the duke and Ljubima.

'Sorry. I forgot my pack and my binnaduria.'

He grabbed them and ran for the door.

'Nine. Ten.'

Both barrels of the pistol fired. But Mochtar had fled into the night.